THE
MAZE

THE MAZE

ELIZABETH
HAWKINS

ORCHARD BOOKS

To Mike

ORCHARD BOOKS
96 Leonard Street, London EC2A 4RH
Orchard Books Australia
14 Mars Road, Lane Cove, NSW 2066
ISBN 1 85213 782 7 Hardback
ISBN 1 85213 854 8 Paperback
First published in Great Britain 1995

A CIP catalogue record for this book
is available from the British Library.
Printed in Great Britain

· CHAPTER ONE ·

Andrew scraped the sodden spikes of hair out of his eyes and crouched down, his back to the rain. A thin, gangly boy, his sandy hair hung over his face in darkened rats' tails. He moulded and squeezed the dried leaves and mud into a wedge.

Slap! He threw the handful against the walls of the dam. The lake was spreading beautifully, out into the road now. The gutter drain, midway down Talgarth Road, was blocked and he and Ben had been working most of the afternoon creating the lake and the dam.

"If it goes on like this," gasped Ben as he dumped another handful of mud and leaves, "we can give the swimming pool a miss this holiday. We've got our own here ... Watch out!"

A car came up the hill and drove straight through the dam. Water poured from the lake like a mountain torrent down Talgarth Road.

"Dam buster!" yelled Ben, shaking a fat fist after the departing car. "Vandal! Come on, Andrew, let's plug the hole."

Andrew wiped the muddy spray from his face with his wet sleeve. "I can't."

"Come on! Ten minutes won't hurt."

"It's my sister's birthday. Mum's putting on a surprise supper and I said I'd be back to blow up the balloons."

"Balloons! Lots of little girls in party dresses then?" Ben spoke without looking up from the drain he was prodding with a stick.

"Not Bella – Joanna."

"Your big sister? She's a bit old for that sort of thing, isn't she?"

Andrew thought so too, but he hadn't liked to tell Mum. Joanna was fourteen now.

"A real family party," Mum had said. "But we'll make it a surprise. Promise me you'll be back by half past five to blow up the balloons."

Dad had promised to get back in time. He'd been working Saturdays recently, but he had faithfully promised Mum to be back.

Andrew looked at his watch – 6.23.

"Didn't I ask you to be back by five-thirty at the latest? Can't you remember one thing for me?"

It was unfair. Andrew had said he was sorry, but Mum couldn't keep off him. Anything he did wrong these days, she never let it pass, but went on and on about it.

"And you'd better go and dry your hair with a towel in the bathroom. And take off those wet clothes – and shoes. I don't want mud on your new bedroom carpet."

In his mind Andrew answered back and told Mum what he thought, but he could never bring himself to do it to her face. Joanna answered back and shouted and got cross, but five minutes later she'd have her arms round Mum or her head against Mum's shoulder, until Mum's strained face relaxed in a smile.

"Do they look all right, Andrew?" Mum said anxiously as he emerged from his room. Andrew hadn't realised how cold he'd got. In dry clothes he felt warm and friendlier towards his mother.

She was staring up at the balloons, decorated with Father Christmases, that hung over the supper table. "It's old stock, but Dad has taken away all his new stock."

The old Christmas balloons looked ridiculous in July.

"Why has Dad taken the stock out?" said Andrew. "It should be in the hall cupboard. I'll find it for you and blow up some better ones."

Mum stared at him, a strange expression in her blue eyes. She wasn't wearing her pink lipstick. She always put on lipstick for special occasions.

"There's no stock. It's gone. I found this stuck at the back, forgotten. You haven't told me if they look all right."

It wasn't like Mum. She always tried to look nice for a special occasion. Her soft, honey-coloured hair was all frizzed up and uncombed. Andrew never bothered to comb his hair himself until his mother forced him to, but he didn't like Mum to be like that too. Was she that cross with him for being late, or was something else wrong?

"Dad will be back any minute. I'll tie these snowmen balloons on the letter box if you like. You can get ready."

But his mother sat down wearily in Dad's chair at the table. There was the cold barbecued chicken Joanna loved, crisps, baked potatoes, baby tomatoes, a salad, and in the middle stood a sticky chocolate cake with candles, Joanna's favourite cake, made by Mum. It looked delicious, but – Andrew wasn't sure if he was so starving that he was imagining it – it seemed a leaner feast than usual.

Andrew tied the balloons to the letter box, and peered out of the porch. The rain was still pelting down. At the bottom of the road he could make out a cluster of bright umbrellas. A squeal of laughter reached him faintly on the wind and then a red umbrella broke away, with two figures beneath it, one large and one small.

Andrew could hear the giggling as Joanna tugged Bella up the hill with one hand and waved the red umbrella in the other. Joanna was like Dad. Everyone laughed when she was around.

"They're coming, Mum," Andrew called, shutting the door.

She had taken off her apron and put on her pink lipstick. She'd forgotten her hair, though.

"Does Bella know about the party?" said Andrew. At least Bella would like the Father Christmases.

"Of course not, Andrew. She'd only tell." Mum sounded cross.

I only asked, said Andrew to himself. "Where's Dad? He's late."

"He's working. He will be late."

"Late? He promised . . ."

"Like you," Mum sighed. She got up and went into the kitchen.

That's not fair, Andrew thought, at least I'm here.

The doorbell rang and rang as the letter box flap went up and down. Bella was giggling and Joanna's voice sang, "Jingle bells, jingle bells, jingle all the way . . ."

One of the snowmen balloons on the door popped and Bella screamed.

Mum rushed smiling and laughing from the kitchen to the front door.

"Look at that chocolate cake! All for me! Barbecued chicken, baked potatoes. Where's the avocado and sour cream dip, Mum?"

Joanna grabbed Mum and hugged her. A sturdy girl with brown, unruly curls, she was taller now than their slight mother. "Where's the dip, Mum?"

"I couldn't get it."

"But they had avocados at the shop on the corner. I saw them. I'll go and get some."

Mum turned away but Andrew saw the smile slip from her face. She looked tired out. "I haven't got the money."

Joanna looked puzzled.

"I want the dip. We always have it on special treats with baked potatoes. Go on, Mum, why can't we?" moaned Bella. She squeezed her dark eyelashes tight over her round blue eyes. Given half a chance she'd force a few tears out.

"Shut up, Bella," hissed Andrew.

"Why should I? You're not the boss." The blue eyes flashed open angrily and then misted over.

Now he'd done it. His little sister's mouth trembled on the verge of tears, tears of frustration at not getting what she wanted and tears of anger with Andrew. Trust him to spoil the party atmosphere.

Then Joanna glanced at the table, looked up and grinned. "Hey, Mum, where's the turkey and Christmas pudding? It's meant to be Christmas, isn't it?"

Mum laughed and Bella started to giggle about the Father Christmas balloons.

"Let's eat," said Mum. "It's no use waiting for Dad. He's going to be late."

"He could have made the effort for my birthday. I can't wait for him. Sue and the girls are taking me out to the cinema this evening. I told you, Mum. Didn't you tell Dad?"

Their mother waited until they had all sat down before answering. Andrew watched the neat features struggle to compose themselves into a smile, but her blue eyes, smaller than Bella's, were distant and wary. Carefully she unfolded her Seasons Greetings paper napkin and laid it across her lap. "He's got to work."

"He needn't think I'll come to his birthday supper. I'll stay in my room doing homework. I'll make a sloppy chocolate mousse and chuck it in his face when he comes to find me . . ."

Bella started giggling again.

"And we'll get the hose from the garden, won't we, Bella, and offer to spray him down to wash it off–"

"And – and – he'll be soaking wet!" shrieked Bella. "And Mum will be cross with him for getting his jacket wet."

"We'll have to chuck him in the dryer," said Joanna through a mouthful of chicken.

Mum was laughing too much to remind Joanna not to talk with her mouth full.

Andrew wished he could be more like Joanna. She wasn't particularly clever, or especially pretty. Just an ordinary sort of girl, a bit on the hefty side, with freckles and a shock of dark hair, but if you looked into the brown eyes they caught and held your attention. They shone with a life all their own, never still – dancing eyes, laughing eyes. In any crowd people moved closer to Joanna, as if warming their cold hands at an irresistible heater. Where she was, there was chatter and laughter and warmth – just like Dad.

"This is from Dad and me," said Mum. She pulled a tiny packet from the side of her plate and pushed it towards Joanna.

"This had better be good," said Joanna fiddling with the tiny parcel to get the paper off. "It couldn't be much smaller . . . Oh, Mum! Is it really mine? Is it for me?"

On the table lay an oval gold locket and chain. The front was etched with twining flowers and vines. Andrew recognised it immediately. It was the locket that Mum wore when she went out with Dad. It had been Grandma's and their great-grandmother's before that.

"Mum, don't you want it any more?"

Joanna tried to wrest open the back with her thumbnail, but it wouldn't open.

"You do it for me, Andrew."

Andrew carefully worked his nail into the crack and prised the back open. Inside was a picture of a toddler, plump and laughing on Dad's knee.

"Look, it's me with Dad," laughed Joanna. "I never knew you had that in there, Mum." Joanna reached across the table and grabbed Mum's hands and kissed them noisily. "Thank you, Mum. I love you and I promise I'll tidy my bedroom and remember to hang the towels up in the bathroom every day and . . ."

Andrew held the locket for Bella to look. Of course he wasn't born then, but he felt a stab of jealousy. He wished he'd been there on Dad's knee.

"Open my present!" Bella shouted excitedly.

Inside Bella's parcel was the purple scarf with orange stripes she had brought from a bargain box at the market. Andrew had tried to persuade her to look at a blue one but she wouldn't.

"Wow!" said Joanna. "Purple and orange!" She tied the scarf round her neck, where it clashed horribly with her red sweatshirt.

"I'll wear it tonight. What do you think, Andrew? Bet I'll need a bodyguard to fight the boys off."

And she would wear it, Andrew knew. If he was her he wouldn't be seen dead in it. He wouldn't risk being laughed at. "I'll go and get my present. I couldn't wrap it."

His heart beating with excitement, Andrew went to his room and pulled the polished wooden pole with spiky arms set on a round base out from under his bed. He felt it. He'd only finished varnishing it the night before. It was dry.

Downstairs again, he stood the base on the table, in front of Joanna. His sister frowned. "What is it?"

Mum looked anxiously at Andrew. "It looks like my mug stand," she said with a nervous little laugh.

"I got the idea from your mug stand. It's to put your bracelets and necklaces on."

For weeks he had heard Mum going on about the tangle of necklaces Joanna had abandoned on her bedroom floor – "just asking to be stepped on and broken". He'd found an old pine broom handle for the stem, Mr Eccles at school had let him have a few small bits of pine lying around the craft room for the arms, and the base was from a broken wooden lamp he'd found in a skip. Andrew was pleased with it. It was one of the best things he'd made.

"It's brilliant! It's just what I need! And you made it, didn't you?" Joanna leant over and gave him a noisy, slobbering kiss.

"Get off!" exclaimed Andrew. But he didn't mind. He looked up and caught Mum smiling.

"Look," said Joanna. "I can hang the locket here, and I can even tie my gorgeous scarf round the top."

The doorbell rang. Joanna looked at her watch and screamed, "They're here! I've got to go."

"What about your birthday cake?" said Mum.

"Mum," pleaded Joanna, "I can't let them down. They're treating me and I'm so full I couldn't eat a crumb. Let's have it for breakfast with Dad."

Mum shrugged her shoulders. "All right. Back by ten now."

"Thank you for the lovely presents." Joanna blew a kiss from the door. "My scarf, I've forgotten my scarf!" she cried in mock horror. She rushed back to pull it off the stand, draped it round her neck and in a flash of orange and purple was gone. The front door opened briefly to chattering voices and slammed shut.

The room was suddenly very quiet and empty.

Andrew opened his eyes. A beam of light from the street lamp outside poured through a crack in the curtains, casting a line of light across his bedroom to the door. Outside he could hear the rain pattering on the window panes.

Andrew loved lying in his warm bed listening to the rain. It reminded him of the family's camping holiday, when the rain had beat on the canvas tent, making the inside feel snug and safe.

But tonight he had woken uneasy, his heart thumping. The beating of the rain couldn't mask the noise beneath him – a murmur of angry voices in the room below.

Sometimes his parents had a row. Andrew's room was at the front, over the living room, and the sound of an argument always woke him. He hated it. He would bury his head in his pillow until he could go to sleep again, and by morning the row was usually over and his parents relaxed and calm after the storm. Once his mother had caught him at the top of the stairs, listening.

"Sometimes Dad and I disagree and we have to clear the air," she had said. "It's always better to get it out of the way."

Andrew didn't believe that of his quiet and calm mother. It was Dad. He was the one who shouted, who blew his top, just like Joanna, yet he was always the fun parent, the lively one who could never be boring or dull.

But tonight it wasn't Dad's voice he heard. It was Mum's voice that was raised in anger.

Slowly, Andrew stretched one foot to the ground. He brought the other to join it and stood up. The board in the centre of the room creaked as he stepped on it, but no one seemed to notice below. On and on went the deep murmur, and the high angry tones. Through the door to the top of the stairs Andrew crept, positioning himself where the banister met the wall. The door into the living room was ajar.

"Why France? Why do you have to go abroad to find work?" came Mum's despairing voice.

"Listen, love, I've tried to explain. There's no work here that pays as well. The fellow at the Rugby Club who's out there says if you work weekends as well you can make a fortune."

"You're too old to be doing heavy labour on sites," said Mum. "It's a job for a young man. There's a lot of men injure themselves doing work like that. Why can't you act your age and be sensible for once?"

"Be sensible! I can't afford to be sensible. I've lost a lot of money."

"We can sell the house. We only just manage the mortgage as it is."

"I'd planned on that already."

"You'd planned on us losing the house . . ." gasped Mum "How much have you lost then?"

Andrew couldn't make out Dad's reply, as it was drowned by Mum's cry.

"Listen, Susan. You'll have to sell it, and find us a flat."

Andrew heard Mum sobbing quietly. "I'll have to sell some of our furniture. We've got too much for a flat."

"Don't make it worse for me," groaned Dad. "I'd stay and do it, but every week I'm here I'm losing money. I'm so sorry, Susan. I know I've wrecked our lives."

Andrew strained over the banister to make out the silence that followed. A nose was blown and then his mother sighed.

"We'll manage," she said quietly. "Joanna will help. She likes a challenge."

Andrew thought about Mum. She liked to know where her things were, liked to plan in advance; she liked sameness, just as he did.

"I knew you'd come up trumps, Susan. And Andrew will be with you too – he'll help," said Dad.

"Not Andrew. He's always got his head in a book, or sits in his room working on his models. He won't like it one bit."

Someone was getting up and moving to the door. "I must pack," said Dad.

Andrew fled. He leapt into bed and buried his head in his pillow.

Dad couldn't have lost his job, because he worked for himself. He was a salesman who bought hardware stock, like brushes, buckets and saucepans, from the manufacturers and sold them to the local shops that needed it. The business had been building up steadily and they'd all been so proud when Dad had announced they could take on a mortgage for a house of their own.

It hadn't surprised Andrew. In the holidays he sometimes helped Dad out on his rounds. He had seen the shopkeepers' tired faces light up when they saw Dad walk in. Dad recorded every name in his black notebook and details such as whether anyone in their family was ill, so that he could ask next time. He made them laugh and look forward to his visits.

"Andrew, you're not asleep, are you?"

Andrew rolled over. The light on the landing framed his father's broad shoulders.

"I've not seen anyone sleep with their face smothered by a pillow and survive it."

Andrew laughed and sat up. "Dad ... I heard. You're going away."

"Yes, son. I'm in a real mess."

"Why?" Andrew couldn't believe that his large, strong, laughing father, who worked so hard to build up his business, could possibly be in a mess.

"It's a tale, but I want you to know. Will you listen?"

"Yes," said Andrew simply.

"Move over then."

The bed creaked under Dad's weight. He was a big man. He'd played rugby until a few years ago when his business became too demanding. Now his bulk was softening over his stomach into a belly. As a little boy Andrew had marvelled at Dad's size. The noisy, laughing hulk of raven-haired man had seemed like a rock to whom his family and customers had clung like comfortable limpets. Andrew knew he would never be like his father. He had the slight build and sandy hair and freckles of his mother's family.

Dad stared at the wallpaper above Andrew's head and rubbed his knees with his hands.

"You see, I had this tremendous idea for making us a windfall, enough to pay off a slice of the mortgage and give us a decent holiday for once. God knows, Mum and I had earned it."

Andrew sat taut, staring at his father's broad chest. "Yes."

"Well, you don't need me to tell you how the shops order their bits and pieces for the summer season – garden chairs, wheelbarrows, buckets and spades and the like. I used to work on each order separately . . ." He paused as if to search for the exact words he needed.

"This company I hadn't dealt with before approached me, said if I could do a sizeable bulk order, I'd get a big discount. I'd make a heck of a lot of money if I could get the shopkeepers to be part of a bulk order."

"But why would they want to, Dad?"

"Good thinking! I'd pass on some of the discount to the shopkeepers as an incentive."

It sounded all right to Andrew. "What . . .?"

"What went wrong? They bought the idea all right –

they trusted me. I collected the money because the deal was that I pay upfront to get the goods."

"Did you know the company, Dad?"

"That's just what I should have asked myself. I didn't find out enough. They're only based fifteen miles from here and I was sure they wouldn't con a local salesman." The shoulders of the broad back were rounded and drooping.

"And – did they?"

His father seemed to shrink on the bed as he looked at Andrew. Then he sank his head in his hands. "They went bust. They must have had financial problems and were desperate for business. That's why they made such a good offer."

"Did you get the stock in time?"

Dad lifted his head and laid a large hand on Andrew's shoulder. "Lost the stock. Lost the money . . ."

"But it wasn't your money."

"No. And those shopkeepers out there – they're not big operators. They're small people and a loss like this can tip them over the edge into impossible borrowing and debt. They've got to have their money back. If they don't, I can write my business off. No one will trust me again."

"I see." Andrew was proud of his father and he wished he could say it, but he couldn't find the right words.

"Look after the girls when I'm gone. Mum says she'll see if the library will take her on full-time for the school holidays."

"Look after Joanna," laughed Andrew. "She'll look after the lot of us whether we like it or not."

"Don't underestimate yourself, son. Joanna's got too much of me, buckets of go and noise and fooling. The likes of us are always at the head of the crowd but we're headstrong at times – we're in too much of a hurry. That's when the mistakes happen. When the going gets tough, it's people like you we need. Folk who think before they leap, who make decisions thoughtfully and who never give up."

Andrew said nothing. He couldn't think what to say. His father, always laughing, the centre of attention wherever he went, the big, tempestuous whirlwind of a man, what did this man think of his only son, so very different from himself? It was a question Andrew had long ago buried deep down and tried to hide. Now he knew. He wished he had known before.

"You won't let me down, son." The big hand squeezed his shoulder as his father stood up.

"No," said Andrew. "I won't."

Andrew sat staring at the bowl-shaped dent where his father had sat. Then he smiled and slid down into the warm bed.

· Chapter Two ·

Andrew woke from a heavy sleep at nine o'clock. It was unlike him to sleep late. He stared at the clock on his new bedside table and saw the black hands standing at a right angle.

Andrew loved his bedroom. Before they had bought the house he had had to share a room with Joanna but now at last he had his own room. He'd found an old plank in a skip and some iron brackets in a junk shop. Together he and Mum had measured and sawn the wood into a shelf for his books. He'd only finished painting it last month.

He turned on his back and looked up at the aeroplanes above him. Suspended from the ceiling on strings were all the models he had made. When the door opened the draught twirled the string and the planes looked as if they were flying.

The planes trembled and began to twirl. Andrew glanced at the door. Standing in the doorway was Bella in her pyjamas. Her face was streaked with tears and she was dragging Beagles, her toy dog, by his ear.

"Dad's not here. I can't find Mum." A sob escaped as Bella gulped for air. "I want my breakfast."

"Go and look for her," said Andrew irritably. He turned over to go back to sleep.

"I have – she's gone."

Andrew sank down the bed and pulled the covers up to his ears.

"I want Mum."

The crying was coming fast and furious now. Andrew knew he wouldn't win.

"OK, cry baby, I'll get it," he said as he threw back the bedclothes.

In the kitchen the table was already laid with cereals, bread and jams, with the untouched chocolate cake at the centre.

"Bella, Mum's laid it all out already!" said Andrew furiously.

"Look – I can't read it. What does it say?" Bella pointed to a scrap of paper anchored under the milk jug.

So that was it. Bella wanted him to read the note from Mum. Although Bella could read a printed book, she couldn't yet decipher ordinary handwriting.

"I think it says she's gone," she wailed. "Where's she gone? She never goes out before breakfast."

Andrew picked up the message.

Gone for job interview. Back by dinnertime. Start sorting your rooms out for packing. Andrew will explain.

Beside the cereals was last night's evening paper open at the SITUATIONS VACANT page. Someone had circled several of the entries.

"Tell me! What does it say?" Bella's frightened and tear-stained face looked up at Andrew.

"I'll tell you," said Andrew, lifting Bella up and plonking

her on her chair. But we'll eat first and wake Joanna. I'm not telling it all twice over."

Bella had cried a lot more when she heard. "What does it mean? Will they put Daddy in prison?"

Joanna, angry at being woken early on a Saturday morning, had demolished her cereal and toast without a word, listening as Andrew recounted what had happened the night before.

"Don't touch the cake," she said eventually. "We'll wait for Mum . . . and Dad – where is Dad?"

"He must have left already," said Andrew.

"Already? Phew! It must be bad."

Joanna sat there lost in unaccustomed thought, picking at the bits of flaky chocolate on the cake. Then she looked up and grinned. "You ought to see your faces, you two. Enough to make me weep. Boo hoo!"

Bella broke out laughing as Joanna pretended to cry.

"A flat again won't be too bad. We can live closer in to town. Then I can meet my friends and get to the shops and cinema whenever I want to."

"Can I go to the skating rink every day?" asked Bella.

"Twice, three times a day," declared Joanna. "And you could go to the library whenever you want, Andrew, and to that boring model shop. It's not all bad."

But it was bad. Andrew knew it as he listened to the deafening music pouring out of Joanna's room. When she was upset she played her tapes loud enough to blast away all consciousness.

He knew it too as he stood on the stepladder in his room and cut down each plane. He'd found a box from Dad's stockroom, and had layered it with old newspapers. Between each layer he placed a plane. He had no idea when he would see them again. A flat might be too small to display them all.

The door slammed. Mum was back. Andrew slipped into the kitchen and watched her hang up her wet raincoat and shake out her dripping umbrella. She filled the kettle with water and reached for the tea jar.

"Andrew! You shouldn't give me such a shock. You're always creeping around."

"Mum!" shouted Joanna as she pounded down the stairs. She burst into the kitchen smiling. "Did you get the job?"

Mum stood the umbrella next to the cooker and sat down. "Yes," she said quietly.

"Fantastic! Clever Mum. What is it? Are you paid a fortune?" Joanna asked.

"I wish I was," said Mum wearily. "The library haven't the money to take on extra staff for the holidays this year."

"Don't tell me," said Joanna. "Let me guess . . . Supervisor of the swimming pool, glamorous Mum fashion model?"

A ghost of a smile flitted over Mum's face. "Waitress at the Perch House Restaurant. It's lunches, but evening and weekend work too."

Andrew thought quickly. Mum would be out most of the day and evening. Who would look after Bella? If it was Joanna and him, Andrew knew who would be doing most of it. He didn't want Bella trailing round with him and Ben all day. It was OK occasionally, but Bella would be bound to tell all they did.

"Don't you worry, Mum," said Joanna. "We'll keep house, won't we, Andrew? I'm a demon with the vacuum cleaner and I adore shopping. We'll learn cordon bleu meals from a cookery book and we'll be ever so tidy – well, at least Andrew will."

Mum smiled.

Typical Joanna, Andrew thought. Promise the earth, everything easy. But at least she could cheer Mum up – it was more than he seemed able to do.

"No, there's Bella," said Mum. "And I'm not having you two roaming around town unsupervised all summer."

"Oh, Mum!" said Joanna.

"And there won't be a house, or a flat. I've decided to let the house right away. The job gives me a room at the restaurant so we won't need a home until you all start school again. It will save us a fortune in mortgage payments and we can decide whether we need to sell in the autumn."

Bella came out of the living room and stood listening in frightened silence, her eyes passing from face to face as they spoke. "What about me? Can I stay with you, Mum? I'll be ever so good."

Mum bent down and folded her arms round Bella. "No, Bella. You're all going away – to the country."

"The *country*?" Joanna shouted. "Who with? I'm not going if there are no shops and nothing to do . . ."

"Where?" asked Andrew. He felt a flicker of interest. He'd always wanted to try living in the country.

"To stay with Cousin Beatrice."

"Who's she?" asked Andrew.

"I've never heard of her," said Joanna angrily.

"Tell me . . . tell me . . ." whined Bella.

"Beatrice, that *is* kind of you. I don't know what I would have done otherwise."

Mum was on the phone in the living room, surrounded by the cardboard boxes Andrew had collected at the supermarket and which he was now stacking in some sort of order. Joanna had gone off to tell Sue of the disaster. "Won't be a sec, Mum, but I must say goodbye." Bella was playing with Beagles on the floor, explaining that he mustn't be frightened of farm dogs.

"Yes, Joanna is fourteen now, you saw her when she was a baby. You'll like her, she's such fun. The other two are eleven and seven. Bella is a pretty little thing and very happy playing with her toys. And Andrew . . . yes, Andrew . . . of course he's a boy. No, he's not at all rough. Please, Beatrice, I don't want to separate them. He's a quiet boy, no trouble, really he is. We'll talk about it then."

Mum sat down and avoided looking at Andrew. "Well, thank goodness that's all arranged."

"She didn't sound too sure," said Andrew. He went out to fetch two more boxes from the hall.

"Don't be ridiculous, Andrew," called Mum. "I know what I'm doing. She's just unused to children."

Andrew came back into the living room, hidden behind the boxes he was carrying. It was easier talking that way.

"Who is she then? I've never met her."

"She's my second cousin. Her father farmed in Dorset and she took over the farm when he got too old. She wasn't able to get away from the farm much, so she never married and runs the farm alone. She must be fairly rattling around in the old farmhouse." Mum's voice was full of false jollity. "Children for the summer will be just what she needs. It's beautiful there, Andrew, rolling hills and heaths – you'll love it."

Andrew dropped the boxes heavily on the floor. Mum smiled pleadingly at him. Andrew saw in that smile all the effort she was making. She was losing their home, moving into a room over a restaurant for the summer. She would miss them, he knew she would. He forced a smile back. "I expect I'll like it."

Mum sighed and laid her head on her arms on the table. Andrew patted her head as he passed. He wished Dad was here. He felt awkward and useless.

It rained continuously for the next two days as they got ready and packed. It was early afternoon on the third day when Andrew and Joanna took advantage of a break in the rain to rush in and out of the house to the car, carrying an assortment of zip bags and plastic carriers stuffed with soft toys, model-making materials, and cassettes.

Finally Mum emerged with an armful of plastic macs and rubber boots. "I do hope the weather improves for you," she said, getting into the car. "It's such a lovely spot. The weatherman on TV says there's more rain and winds coming and the farmers are getting desperate about the harvest."

"Why?" asked Bella.

Mum turned the ignition in the car. It took a while to start after the torrential rain of the previous night.

"I suppose because the corn won't ripen."

"But plants need water, so rain's good for them," said Bella.

Andrew sat in the back with Bella, his trainers and socks sodden from splashing through the puddles. On his knee he clutched his small box of enamel paints. He didn't trust them to a carrier bag. Mum was chattering on to take their minds off leaving and the last time they would see their home. He'd told himself he wouldn't look back and he didn't, not even as they slid past the blocked drain in Talgarth Road.

"There's sea in Dorset, isn't there? I'm going to swim even if it is raining," said Joanna from the front.

"Even if it's cold and the beach is empty?" put in Bella.

"That's the best time. The water's warmer in than out and the rain comes down like a shower. You get out fast, rub down quickly, into your clothes and you're as warm as a toasted bun."

Mum laughed.

"And I'm going to ask Beatrice if I can help with the harvest. I'm going to get a pitchfork and toss hay on to the back of a cart and ride on the cart back to the farm."

"They don't do it like that any longer," said Andrew. "You've been looking at all those pictures in the history books of girls being sent out to work on farms in the Second World War."

"So, clever boy, how do you know?"

"I've read about it. It's all massive combine harvesters with sealed cabins, with air conditioning and radios and walkie-talkies back to the farm . . ."

"I don't mind," said Joanna. "If it goes on pelting down like this, I can ride in the cabin and listen to music . . ."

"And paint your nails with that red stuff," shouted Bella.

Andrew and Mum laughed.

"You horrible little girl," snarled Joanna, and snapped her teeth at Bella.

But they all felt better.

The drive took longer than Andrew expected. Once they were on the motorway the wind started gusting and sheets of rain pelted against the windscreen. The traffic slowed to a crawl and the windscreen wipers had to work overtime to clear both the rain and the spray thrown up by a lorry in front. By the time Mum turned off the motorway on to quieter, country roads they were all tired.

Andrew peered out of the window. The land around was undulating. In fields, sodden sheep munched grass or wretched-looking cows lay down in the shelter of a tree. Other fields were sown with greeny-yellow corn, with patches here and there flattened by the wind and rain. The hedgerows speeding past glistened with wet leaves under the forbidding grey skies. Dull greens and greys and browns stretched out as far as he could see. It wasn't how he'd thought of the country. It looked dismal.

"Two miles now, I reckon," said Mum. "If I remember

rightly, it's through this wood and over the brow of the hill."

In front, the lane disappeared into a dark canopy of overhanging trees. The car climbed sluggishly up the hill into the wood.

"What's that?" said Mum suddenly.

Andrew heard a rattling beneath the car. Then there was a clatter and a terrible screeching noise. "Stop, Mum!" he shouted.

The car came to a halt to the sound of metal scraping the ground.

"Don't worry, Mum," said Joanna. "I was feeling sick anyway. You tell me where the farm is and I'll run on and call the AA."

"It will take them ages to get out here," sighed Mum. "We'll be late for tea with Beatrice and then I've got the long drive back."

"I'll look," said Andrew.

He stepped out into a slush of mud and wet grass. He peered under the car – nothing wrong at the front. He moved round to the back. He should have guessed it! One of the clamps holding the silencer to the chassis had rusted and broken off. The silencer was trailing on the ground.

"I've got some wire in my box, Mum. Let me have a try. Maybe I can fix it up for the time being."

"I want to do a wee, I want to do a wee," started Bella, writhing on the back seat.

"Can't you wait?" said Mum. "We're almost there."

"I can't, I can't," whined Bella. "Not if Andrew tries to mend the car."

"I'll take her behind a tree somewhere," said Joanna. "If I'm not going to get my trek to the farm, we can go exploring, can't we, Bella?"

Joanna grabbed Bella by the hand and they set off up a narrow footpath into the woods. Relieved to be out of the car, the girls flung back their heads to catch the rain in their mouths.

"Don't go far and get soaked," called Mum. "I don't want to have to come and fetch you."

It was difficult to get to the silencer. Andrew tried lying on one of the plastic macs, but he still got wet and muddy. His hands were covered in oil, which made it difficult twining the slippery wire round the hot metal cylinder. But he was enjoying himself. He hoped it would work and then Mum could write and tell Dad.

"Are you all right under there, Andrew?" Mum's face appeared upside-down at the bottom of the car. "I'd send Joanna to phone for the AA but the naughty girls aren't back yet."

Andrew wriggled out from under the car. "I think it should hold till you get back. Take the car into the garage tomorrow."

"Look at you, Andrew," said Mum. "Here – clean yourself up with these hankies."

The paper tissues seemed to smear the mud and oil around his hands and arms more than clean it off.

"Where are those girls? I told them not to be long."

"I'll go and get them," said Andrew.

He threw the box of tissues into the back of the car and started up the track. The rain had stopped. He hadn't noticed it underneath the car. The grey clouds overhead were parting and here and there streaks of blue were breaking through. Rays of sunlight filtered through the wet branches of the trees so that the wetness around sparkled in the brilliant light.

Andrew had hardly gone more than a few yards when, above him, out of a dense area of trees, walked Joanna. Bella trailed behind her.

"Wait for me!" Bella shouted. "Wait for me, Joanna!"

"Where *have* you been?" said Andrew when Joanna was close. "Mum's been getting into a state."

Joanna walked past him without a word. She looked pale and preoccupied.

"Joanna – are you all right?" said Andrew.

"Just a bit car sick, I expect," said Mum. "I'd forgotten it was so far. Look at this sun . . . What a treat. I'd never have thought the weather would change so quickly. Now get in, all of you."

"Joanna?" Andrew said uncertainly.

Joanna turned at the car door. The sun fell full on her face, so that must have been why her brown eyes stared so dully at Andrew, and yet he had the impression that she was not looking at him but through and beyond him.

"You might have waited for Bella," said Andrew for want of anything better to say.

· Chapter Three ·

The farmhouse ranged alongside the lane. Its walls were of old red brick and the windows were small. Water streamed from a broken gutter, down a wall striped with slimy moss, to what passed for a garden below.

Tall white daisies struggled with nettles and creeping brambles, and here and there an ancient rose bush offered up a faded flower.

"Here we are," said Mum with a note of false gaiety as she turned the car into a gateway. The rusty iron gate tilted drunkenly open. Andrew saw that the top hinge was broken.

"It's changed a bit since I was last here," said Mum. An anxious note had crept into her voice.

In front of them lay a sea of mud. The farmyard was bordered by the house on one side, and on the other two sides by low brick barns. Black holes gaped in the barn roofs where tiles had fallen off and not been replaced.

All three children stared in silence.

From out of the house stepped a figure wrapped like a bundle in an ancient man's mac, feet shod in rubber boots. Mum ran down her window. "Beatrice! It's been such a long time."

The bundle held up a warning hand. "Don't bring that

car in here. The mud's that bad we'll need a tractor to get it out again."

"Andrew," whispered Mum. "Get the bag with the boots out from the back. We'll ruin our shoes if we step out in this."

"I don't like my boots," whined Bella.

"Shut up," said Andrew, but he understood. Bella had never complained about her boots before. She just didn't want to stay.

Without a word Joanna pulled on her boots and stepped out of the car ahead of Mum.

A thin face with taut, high cheekbones, framed with wispy grey hair, stared at Joanna. "You must be Joanna."

Andrew had somehow thought Cousin Beatrice would be the same age as their mother, but she was an old woman. Her face crinkled into a smile, but Joanna was gazing silently up at the farmhouse. What had got into her? She was never at a loss for a word or a laugh. If she was depressed then they would all be depressed.

"And this little girl must be Bella." A veined hand, with gnarled knuckles, reached out and stroked Bella's shiny blonde curls. Bella clung to her mother, her mouth quivering.

Someone had to say something. Usually Andrew stood back and let Joanna hold forth, but the girls seemed dumb-struck with disappointment.

"I'm Andrew," he said and stepped forward. He held out his hand.

The crinkled smile faded as Cousin Beatrice's eyes darted

down to his hand. It was covered with oil and mud. Andrew had forgotten what he must look like after lying under the car. The old lady appeared to nod vaguely, but didn't shake his hand. Instead, she turned to lead them into the kitchen. Andrew pulled a face at Joanna, willing her to do her bit. She ignored him.

"I said I wouldn't have the boy."

They were sitting in the wide kitchen, beneath a low ceiling criss-crossed with old beams. A packet of ginger biscuits lay open on the pine table in front of them, beside a large, brown teapot.

"But, Beatrice ... I don't know who I can ask to have him all summer. I don't want to separate them. It's not easy for us at the moment."

Bella huddled up against her mother while Joanna stared out of the dusty window. Andrew didn't want to stay. He knew that. Not where he wasn't wanted.

The old woman pulled herself up from the table and limped over to the cooking range along the wall. A black dog, lying in an old wicker basket, thumped his tail, then stood up and yawned. Beatrice refilled the teapot from the black kettle. "I'm not having the boy. I've not had a boy or man stay in this house since Father died – and I never will."

The dog followed her to the table. She held out her hand to its head, but it walked past and slumped at Andrew's feet. Andrew patted the soft, sleek head and the dog's tail thumped on the sheets of old newspaper spread across the stone-flagged floor.

"Don't feed him," snapped Beatrice. "I'll not have Sam fed from the table."

"I wasn't," said Andrew defensively.

Beatrice glared at him.

"He's a quiet boy, no trouble, Beatrice, and he's very handy at mending things. He's just done such a good job on the broken silencer. If you've got any little repair jobs round the place Andrew'd be only too pleased to help."

Andrew stared into his teacup. He was being sold. He wasn't wanted, so he was being sold instead.

Beatrice grunted as if she didn't believe it.

"And he can get up a ladder and fix all sorts of things."

His mother gazed out of the window at the barns with their decrepit roofs. Andrew took in the dripping tap at the old china sink, and the crumbling plaster hole where a towel rail must once have been. Mum was crafty.

It was true. He was good at mending things and he enjoyed it but he was blowed if he would do anything to help Cousin Beatrice.

Beatrice sat examining the teapot. From time to time she glanced up at Andrew with a hostile, calculating stare. Slowly she drummed her fingers on the table in the expectant silence.

"I'll try him out," she said at last. "He can stay for a few days and we'll see how it goes. Mind you – he'll have to work for his keep."

Andrew held open the car door as their mother got in. The

girls stood on the kitchen step, Joanna watching, Bella clutching Beagles and waving.

"I'm sorry, Andrew," said Mum. "She's just funny about men. She never liked Dad and I wouldn't come to see her without him. That's why we've not been in touch."

"You could have told me," said Andrew coldly.

"I was sure once she'd met you she would like you. Try, please, Andrew. I'm sure you can bring her round."

"If she speaks to me like that, I'm not lifting a finger."

"Please, Andrew . . . I can see she's already upset poor Joanna – she's hardly said goodbye to me. I know it's my fault, but what else can we do?" She was close to tears.

"OK, Mum," Andrew said. "I'll try."

"Isn't it pretty," exclaimed Bella. Her tears at saying goodbye to her mother were forgotten as she ran ahead, exploring the old house. They were in the 'best' bedroom. "You are lucky, Joanna. It's like a bedroom in an old film on telly . . . Joanna, are you listening to me?"

Joanna stared at the high wooden bed, the low old-fashioned dressing table with its flowery curtain pulled round its drawers and its matching stool. The walls were lined with a rosebud wallpaper, broken in the far wall by a low window. Its wide sill was a seat, scattered with faded satin cushions.

"My mother's room," explained Beatrice with obvious pride. "I never use it. My mother was a lady, but I'm a worker, a farmer – too mucky for a room like this."

"Some lady you are!" said Andrew, nudging Joanna. "You'll never live up to it." Andrew was neat by habit and he laughed at the prospect of Joanna's careless untidiness.

"Leave her alone, boy," said Beatrice sharply. "While you're in my house I'll have none of that behaviour."

What behaviour? He was only teasing Joanna.

Joanna smiled and said nothing. Yet she was usually the first person to leap to the defence if one of them was unfairly accused.

Bella's room was the old nursery. It had a small truckle bed in the corner, painted with a daisy-chain pattern. A knotted rug of faded rainbow colours lay on the floor, while on the walls were tiers of shelves packed with old toys and books.

"Look, Joanna, a rocking horse and a Noah's ark with all the animals. Oh no, the camel's leg is broken. Look, Andrew."

Andrew took the camel, beautifully carved from one piece of wood. "I'll make a new leg. I can stick—"

"No you won't," interrupted Beatrice. She held out her hand for the camel and set it back on a high shelf. "You will not touch anything here without my permission. In fact you may not go into the girls' rooms."

"But what if Bella wants me to play with her, or she's homesick?" said Andrew. He didn't anger easily but he recognised the heat creeping through his body.

"Bella can come to me, or Joanna can keep her company. I'm not having rough boys' play in these rooms."

There was no room prepared for Andrew.

"You can sleep in the attic. You will keep it tidy. If my hip feels better in the morning I'll come and check."

Beatrice gave him a pile of old sheets and blankets from the oak cupboard on the landing. Andrew picked up his bags and climbed the narrow staircase to the attic.

"Wait for me! I'm coming too!" shouted Bella.

"Stay in your room, dear," said Beatrice as she closed the doors of the tall cupboard and limped to the stairs leading down to the kitchen, "or come with me. We can sort the eggs."

"I'll stay," called Bella cheerfully.

As Andrew wrestled with the stiff door at the top of the attic stairs, he heard Bella close behind him.

"I've taken my shoes off. She won't hear," said Bella. "I like my room. I can't wait to see yours."

The door swung open. It was several minutes before Andrew could make out anything in the gloom. The room was covered in dust, from its bare wooden floor to the sheets that lay over the few bits of furniture.

"Oh!" said Bella in disappointment, and she wrinkled up her nose. "I'm going to sneeze."

A faded light came through a low gable window set deep between sloping walls. Andrew walked across and rubbed the glass with his sleeve. A fresh beam of sunlight penetrated the room. He moved round quickly, whisking the dust sheets off a rusting brass bed, a straight-backed wooden chair, a chest of drawers and a table with a china washbowl and jug on it.

"This must have been a maid's room," said Andrew. "But they can't have had a maid for years and years."

"It feels cold," said Bella. "You can't stay here, look."

Bella pointed to the ceiling. Dark patches of speckled mould spread out from a beam above.

"The rain's been coming in," said Andrew. "There must be a leak."

"You can share my room," said Bella. "It's very big and we can put blankets on the floor . . ."

"No," said Andrew and he gave her a hug. "Beatrice wouldn't let me. She's really got it in for me, the old cow, and I don't want you in trouble too."

He'd clean the place up. It wouldn't ever be homely but it had potential. If he could get the window open and let in the sunlight there would be interesting patches of light and shade under the sloping roof and the beams would be great for pinning aeroplanes to.

If he wasn't welcome, he could see the advantages of being up in the attic in a world of his own.

"Joanna, we've got to help him. It's cold and dusty," said Bella, when they went back to report to Joanna.

Joanna was sitting on her window seat, staring out at the woods high on the hill.

"It's not fair on Andrew," Bella continued. "He's got a horrid room. It's dirty and cold. Let's go and ask Beatrice for some cleaning things."

Joanna hardly seemed to register Bella's plea.

"Joanna, are you listening?" cried Bella, pulling at her arm.

Joanna stared briefly at Bella and Andrew before turning away again. "He can do it himself," she said.

"Why are you so horrid, Joanna?" cried Bella. "I'll help you, Andrew."

Andrew watched Joanna in amazement. What was wrong with this place? Joanna was never as mean as this.

"Thanks, Joanna, thanks very much," he said angrily. "And you can carry your own bags up."

"Don't quarrel," said Bella tearfully.

She followed Joanna's gaze as she stared out at the woodland bathed in the golden sunlight of evening. "I thought it was awful when we arrived," Bella said, "but it's fun exploring and look – it's all pretty outside now. It is, isn't it? Talk to me."

"Yes – it is," said Joanna dully.

"That box of paints – I've seen it. I'm not having them in the house," said Beatrice coldly as Andrew and Bella went into the kitchen. She stared disdainfully at him, dust from cleaning the attic room now added to the mud and oil from the car. "And that carrier bag with the wood and saw and chisel. You can't bring that in the house."

"I've got to put it somewhere."

"Put it in the barn. If you want to use it, be sure to stay there, out of the house."

Andrew picked up the box of paints and his modelling

bag. He gritted his teeth and remembered Mum's worried face and Dad's hand on his shoulder.

"I'll come and check," said Beatrice, wiping her hands on her apron. "And I need to show you where you do your evening chores."

The barn was the furthest building across the sea of mud. It was dark inside and full of musty smells. In a minute or two Andrew's eyes grew accustomed to the gloom, helped by light seeping in from a hole in the roof. He put his things down on an old iron anvil that must once have been used by a blacksmith.

"Leave them," said Beatrice. "Follow me. The wood for the log basket is stacked behind the barn, and the coal, from the bunker next to the logs, goes into the coal scuttle beside the range. After that, take the milk bottles from outside the back door down to the gate and put them in the milk box. I don't keep cows any longer."

When Andrew had fetched the fuel and got rid of the milk bottles, he reported back to the kitchen.

"You're not finished yet," declared Beatrice as he pulled out a chair. "There's the chickens in the orchard to drive into the pen and mind you shut them in securely for the night."

Andrew wasn't going to ask Beatrice how you drove chickens in, but he was glad to be out again, doing something on his own. He would have preferred a friend with him, though; he thought back wistfully to all the plans he and Ben had made for the summer holiday.

The orchard lay behind the older, thatched wing of the

farm. The spreading apple trees and tall pear trees were old, their branches a tangled mass of twigs. One apple tree had collapsed to the ground, but apples were still growing on its leafy branches. About ten brown chickens, pecking among the early windfalls, squawked at the sight of Andrew. A proud cock with a red comb strutted about among them.

"Wait for me!" Bella called at the gate. "I got out when Beatrice went up to see Joanna. Aren't they beautiful? Is that a cock?"

Before Andrew could stop her, Bella reached to touch the blue-black tail feathers on the rear of the strutting cock. The bird flashed round and pecked her on the leg. Bella screamed as blood trickled down her leg.

"It's all right. It's only a scratch," said Andrew, dabbing at the shallow cut with an oily tissue.

But Bella cried and cried and clung to Andrew. "I want Mum. Joanna won't talk to me and Beatrice hates you . . ."

"Shush, Bella. It'll be all right. You like your room, don't you? And you said yourself it was fun exploring. Come on, let's shoo these chickens in."

Andrew and Bella walked back to the yard hand in hand. Bella had enjoyed chasing the chickens, although they gave the cock a wide berth as he paraded in at the rear of the hens.

"How many eggs will there be? I expect the cock lays an enormous egg. They'll probably be brown eggs with brown hens. Beatrice doesn't eat the hens, does she? I don't think she would . . ."

Andrew half-listened to Bella's happy chatter. Mesmerised, he was watching the clouds in the sky turn gold and orange where the sun was setting. You never saw that much of the sky in town.

The farm was L-shaped. He hadn't noticed that before. His room was in the side of the L that was roofed with mossy thatch. Near the roof ridge was a wispy hole, as if an animal had burrowed in. No wonder it leaked. Beneath the thatch was the older part of the farm, with tiny windows peeping out of walls the colour of thick cream.

The side of the farm that fronted the road and the yard was newer, built of brick and roofcd with slates, shining and steaming still from the day's rain. It was a beautiful old farm, even if it was falling to pieces.

"Wait, Bella, watch!"

Andrew pulled a stub of pencil out of his pocket and a small notebook. It was where he jotted down his ideas for new model planes. Turning to a fresh page, he crouched down and drew a plan.

"Look, the farm is shaped like an L. If I put the barns on here it's like another arm to the L, like a T upside-down."

"Like the wings of a bird," said Bella.

"It could be."

"I wish it would fly us home, Andrew, back to Mum!"

· CHAPTER FOUR ·

"Did you set the catch on the gate?" Beatrice asked Andrew when he and Bella returned.

She didn't speak to him again. After supper she bustled round the two girls, showing them faded photographs from a wooden box in the sitting room. It was as if Andrew wasn't there, though Bella kept trying to bring him in.

"Look at this funny one, Andrew. It's Beatrice with Mummy when she was a little girl."

Joanna took each photograph in turn, considered it, and laid it back in the box.

"That locket, my dear," exclaimed Beatrice. "How pretty it looks on you. It's just like the one my grandmother is wearing in this photograph."

Joanna fingered the locket round her neck. She had worn it since they arrived, her hand frequently moving up to it, as if checking it was still there.

"It was great- or great-great-grandmother's," piped in Bella. "Mum gave it to Joanna for her birthday."

Beatrice smiled and leant forward to look more closely, then peered at the brown photograph. "I do believe it's the same one. How lovely!"

Andrew felt like the unwanted guest. Unnoticed, he slipped up to his bedroom. He preferred the company of his books anyway.

He stretched out on the bed, his *Encyclopaedia of Modern Aircraft* in his hands. *In the mid-1950s Northrop started development of its N-156 as a light and easily maintained yet supersonic fighter suitable ...*

He was tired. He stared up at the ceiling and wondered how he would be able to stand it ... The book slid off the bed to the floor.

Andrew jerked upright. It was dark. He'd gone to sleep in his filthy clothes while he was reading. He rescued the book from the floor and laid it on the chair beside the bed.

He crept to the door with his wash bag and tiptoed down the stairs to the bathroom. All the lights in the house were out and the bedroom doors shut. He hesitated outside Joanna's door. He so much wanted to have a chat with her about everything. She'd said hardly a word since they arrived, and he would never have guessed he would miss a cheerful voice so much. But it was too late and he couldn't risk Beatrice catching him in her room. He'd speak to her in the morning.

The pipes in the bathroom gurgled and spluttered. If he had a bath he would wake the whole house. He dabbed his face and hands half-heartedly with a cold flannel, promising himself a good wash in the morning.

The bed felt damp and cold. Andrew sat there hugging his knees, daring himself to lie down.

Somewhere below him a door clicked and a floorboard creaked in the passage. Someone was moving about. It made him feel more alone and isolated in his attic room. Somehow this summer had to be got through. If only he could do something to help Mum and Dad, then maybe they could all get away from here sooner.

As he dozed off he heard the hens squawking: so much for the peaceful countryside. They made enough noise and commotion to match any town street on a Saturday night . . .

Andrew felt more cheerful when he woke in the morning. Sun was streaming in through the small window. He peered out across fields and distant heathland to the hill with its encircling crown of woods. He couldn't wait to go up there with Joanna and explore.

He heard the clatter of pans in the kitchen below as he ran a bath in the huge old tub. Brown water belched and spluttered from the outsize taps, until it ran clearer. He scrubbed at the oil stains on his arms with a scratchy loofah from the metal soap rack that stretched across the bath. Then he wallowed in the giant tub, savouring the bacon smells wafting up from the kitchen.

"The sun's out – we must get out . . . " he announced to the girls as he leapt down the last step into the kitchen. His smile vanished as he met Beatrice's grim face. She frowned as she turned from the range, frying pan in hand.

" . . . after I've helped . . . " Andrew's voice faded away.

Bella's face was white and fearful as she stared at her plate of bacon. Poor Bella, thought Andrew, she's really missing Mum.

Joanna said nothing, but carefully buttered a fresh piece of toast.

Andrew reached for the cornflakes and pulled out a chair.

"Get off that chair."

Beatrice's steely voice had a furious coldness in it.

"Why?" Andrew looked up.

"There's no breakfast for the likes of you. Get your boots on."

Andrew stared in bewilderment at Joanna. As if unaware of his presence, she went on spreading her toast, neatly cutting it up into four pieces. Bella looked as if she was about to say something, but a glance at Beatrice's livid face was enough to make her hesitate.

Andrew was ready to refuse. Why should he be the only one without breakfast? But nobody moved to support him. There was nothing for it – he would have to have his breakfast later.

He crossed to the door and pulled on his boots. Beatrice beckoned and he followed her in silence out into the farmyard. The mud was drying on the surface and fine cracks were appearing.

Sam slunk out, walking close beside Andrew.

"Get back, Sam," ordered Beatrice fiercely. "Back – at once!" Sam slunk back, as if he had known all along it would be futile to follow.

Without a word, Beatrice led Andrew through the yard and into the orchard. Now he saw that the hens' pen was right up close to the wall beneath his window. He wasn't going to get much sleep if they squawked like that every night. It was going to be a bore if he had to collect the eggs before breakfast . . . Surely Beatrice could wait half an hour until he'd eaten.

The gate to the pen was open. Andrew stared in horror. He couldn't believe what he saw. Four hens lay mauled and dead on the ground. There were feathers everywhere. The cock and the three remaining hens cowered in the corner, clucking monotonously with distress.

"A fox," said Beatrice savagely. "A fox got in. You didn't latch the gate."

"I did, I did."

Andrew stared appalled at the carnage before him, and then at Beatrice's quivering face.

"I asked you and you said you had. You lied. You did it on purpose."

"It's the truth, honestly, Beatrice." Andrew's voice rose in desperation. "Ask Bella – she saw me do it."

"Don't bring in the little girl. She's frightened of you. She'll say anything."

"Bella's not frightened of me," said Andrew furiously. "I know I latched the gate. The latch must be loose, it must be the wind or something."

But as he said it Andrew knew it couldn't be that. The latch had been rusty, so he had wedged it tight, and the wind had died down with the rain yesterday afternoon.

"You will collect the carcasses up," said Beatrice. "Clean them and pluck them. At least I can keep them for Sam."

For a moment Andrew thought he heard a sob in her voice. Perhaps she'd had the hens for ages and knew them all.

"I'm sorry, Beatrice, but it wasn't me."

She turned and glared at him. "Sorry, sorry ... It won't cover up lies."

She turned and Andrew followed her back through the yard and into the kitchen. He wasn't sure he felt like breakfast any more after the sight he'd seen.

At the door Andrew kicked off his boots but Beatrice stormed in hers across the kitchen, leaving a trail of muddy clots on the floor. Bella watched, wide-eyed with fear. Joanna smiled as she read from an old newspaper from the floor.

It happened so quickly, Andrew wasn't sure who moved first. From a peg on the wall Beatrice snatched a brown stick and advanced towards Andrew with it high above her head.

"I should never have let your mother leave you," she shouted. "Men! Where there's a man there's always trouble. I should have known."

Bella screamed as the stick came down towards Andrew. He put out his hand and struggled with Beatrice to wrest the stick away from her. He was so furious he didn't care that Beatrice was an old woman. Neither his father nor his mother had ever beaten any one of them. No one would beat him.

"Andrew! Andrew!" shrieked Bella.

Beatrice had fallen back against the wall. Andrew stared in astonishment at the stick in his hand. It was a riding crop, the sort of whip you saw in old-fashioned films – a horse whip.

In front of him Beatrice had collapsed into a cowering heap. A pathetic old woman, she half-lay and half-sat, moaning, with her hands held out in front of her as if to protect herself.

She's expecting me to hit her, it dawned on Andrew. She thinks I'm going to hit her with the whip.

Behind him Bella gasped, and there was the sound of a shrill laugh.

Andrew bent the whip across his knee as far as it would go. It was tough but it was old and dry. With a snap it broke in two. Then in turn he broke the two pieces into four. He strode across the kitchen, lifted the lid of the cooking range and dropped the pieces into the glowing embers below. Pulling on his boots, Andrew stamped out of the kitchen and slammed the door behind him.

It took several minutes for Andrew's eyes to adjust to the darkness in the barn. The sun glaring down in the yard had a blinding quality, while the barn was as dark and cool as a cellar. All he wanted was to be swallowed up for ever in its depths.

His hands trembled at his sides and his breath came in shallow pants. If anything like this happened again he'd run away. He'd find somewhere and somehow to live, even if he had to live rough in the woods. He had a book at home, on surviving in the wild. It had a lot in it about building a bivouac of branches, making fires and finding food.

He laid his hands on the cold iron of the anvil, grasping it as if to steady himself with its chill.

He'd promised Dad to look after the girls, but Joanna wasn't doing her bit. What had got into her?

Andrew remembered the shrill laugh when Beatrice had raised the whip to him. Yes – Bella had gasped, but behind him someone had definitely laughed. It was Joanna.

Andrew shook his head and sat down on an abandoned garden seat. He didn't know Joanna any more. She wasn't like the cheerful, noisy sister he was used to. Leaving the house, the move, had upset her, made her mean and unfriendly. Mum was wrong – Joanna hadn't coped at all with the change or the challenge.

Andrew fished around in his pocket for a packet of mints. He was starving. He couldn't find any, but his hands closed on his notebook. He pulled it out and flipped through the pages. At one end of the bench a beam of sunlight poured through the broken roof. Andrew shifted into the light and inspected the sketches he had made of the farm. He liked the upside-down T-shape of the old and newer sides of the farm and the other wing with the yard and barns. He would make a model of them, a model farmyard, and keep it for Bella's birthday. He could see all sorts of promising materials hanging round the barn – old planks of wood, string, straw.

Andrew's interest began to stir. It would give him something to do, something to keep him sane in this madhouse. He could make the barn his own place and get away from Beatrice and the girls. The summer might be bearable then.

Carefully he unpacked his model-making materials and tools and laid them on an antique table he found against the barn wall. The veneer was cracked and filthy with dirt and cobwebs. He'd have to clean it up a bit before he started work.

He went over to the corner and inspected a stack of old planks. They weren't rotten and he was lucky that there was no sign of worm.

"What are you doing?"

Andrew swung round. In the doorway he could see Joanna's silhouette, dark against the brilliant light outside.

"You can see the kit, can't you? I'm going to make some planes." For some reason Andrew didn't want to tell Joanna what he planned.

"You can't. Beatrice –"

"Beatrice this, Beatrice that. I'm sick of Beatrice. And if you think I'm going to sit in that kitchen with her going on at me like that, you must be nuts."

"Beatrice says –"

"Don't tell me. I'm not listening. Why didn't you say something? You're the oldest, aren't you? You just sit around like ... like some dumb puppet. You know it isn't true. Joanna, you can't believe her," Andrew's voice pleaded. "Why did you laugh?"

"Beatrice says you are to collect up the carcasses, clean them and pluck them."

"Joanna." Andrew strode over to the door. He grabbed her by the shoulders and shook her. "What on earth are you playing at? What's got into you? Where have you gone to ...?"

Where have you gone to? That was it. Andrew stared as Joanna turned away without a word, back across the yard and into the kitchen. Yes, he thought, the Joanna he knew had gone. She was like an empty shell.

Andrew moved back to the table. He looked at his sketches. He no longer felt like doing anything except escaping.

He was still staring blankly when the kitchen door banged again. He looked back just in time to see Joanna walk briskly past the barn door in the direction of the orchard. Joanna never did anything alone. She liked to go out with friends or take Andrew with her. She wasn't a solitary sort of person. Why didn't she call him?

Andrew resisted the urge to follow and pulled out a thin plank of wood. He could get three sections out of it and if he nailed them together tightly, they'd make a good base for the model.

The base was nailed and he began to mark out the shapes of the farm buildings with a ruler and chalk crayon. He'd lost track of the time, he'd become so absorbed in his plan.

"What are you making?"

Andrew hadn't heard Bella slip into the barn.

"It's a secret."

"Is it a plane?"

"No."

"It's going to be a Noah's ark, isn't it? Is it for me?"

"I don't know who it's for yet."

"Beatrice says I can have the Noah's ark in the nursery for ever, so you can sell this one and get lots of money. I've saved my toast for you."

"Thanks, Bella!" Andrew took the proffered piece of toast. Dry and hard now, it smelled delicious to his empty stomach. "Where's Joanna?"

"She's gone exploring and she's left me behind, but I saw her going up the fields. She's mean."

"Where's Beatrice?"

"She's in her bedroom and she's shut the door. I think she's crying. Do old ladies cry?"

The barn base outline didn't fit properly beside the yard.

"Stop pestering me, Bella. Now I've made a mistake."

Bella sat down on the dirt floor, close to Andrew's feet. He wanted to tell her not to bother him, but he hadn't the heart to send her away and he found her physical closeness comforting. Bella fished in her pocket and produced two elephants from the ark and started talking to herself as she played with them under the table. Quietly they both became absorbed in what they were doing.

Andrew had been working steadily, examining his sketches and measuring the outlines, when a raucous car horn jerked them into alertness. Bella ran to the door.

"It's a lorry – really dirty – and there's an old man with a big beard and a boy in it."

"Beatrice – you there?" came a deep, booming Dorset voice. "We've brought the logs."

"About time too, Peter," came Beatrice's voice from the kitchen step. "You said you'd bring them a month ago."

"You've still got plenty. I know that's so, so what's worryin' you? If you want somethin' to worry about look at the harvest – half-rotten in the field it is."

"And I'll need you for that too if this weather holds."

"All in good time. We'll need a good few days of sun to save this lot. I'll be there when I'm needed, and bring the boy to help."

Andrew heard a snort from Beatrice.

"Now don't go on like that, Beatrice, or the boy won't be comin'. You're fortunate enough to have me that'll still work with you."

"And you're lucky to have the work, Peter."

"Dare say I am, dare say I am." A deep chuckle filled the courtyard and the kitchen door slammed.

Bella ran back to Andrew. "It's an old man bringing logs. He's carrying them round to the shed at the back."

Andrew carefully laid a stick of balsa wood over the outside line of the farm wall. He took some tacks from a tin and hammered the strip deftly into position.

"Is the boy his helper?" he asked, curious but unwilling to be torn away from the delicate work of the outlines.

Bella ran back to the door. "He's not really helping. He's sort of being pulled along by the old man."

"Don't be silly, Bella."

"No . . . he's back with the old man and he's carrying logs too now. They've got an awful lot to carry."

Should he help? Andrew wouldn't mind carrying and stacking the logs with the boy, but he sat rooted in front of his model. He wouldn't lift a finger for Beatrice, not until she said she was sorry and treated him like a human being.

Giggles broke out from the door.

"He's trying to carry too many and he keeps on dropping them."

More giggles.

"He's seen me and he's doing it on purpose."

There was a burst of laughter outside and Bella shrieked with delight.

"Stop playing the fool, Simeon," shouted the deep voice. "Pick 'em up. Still, we didn't expect to find a lovely young lady up here, did we?"

"Andrew, did you hear that?" giggled Bella. "He called me a young lady. Ooh . . . Simeon's coming over."

"Who's coming over?"

Andrew turned to look over his shoulder. A boy much his own height stood staring in through the doorway, his arms clasped round a bundle of logs.

"What's your name then?"

For a moment Andrew wondered who the boy was talking to.

"Bella."

The boy turned towards Bella. "That's a nice name. You must be a princess with a name like that."

Bella squealed with delight and Andrew chuckled to himself. It was good to hear Bella so happy. He grinned at the boy but the boy stared back, ignoring Andrew's smile.

What was wrong with everybody here? Andrew was shy with new people – quite the opposite of Joanna who loved fresh faces – yet he made good friends in the end. But here, nobody even wanted to get to know him. He turned back to his model and started tapping tacks briskly into the balsa-wood strips.

Someone was standing beside him. "What are you making?" said the boy.

"A model," said Andrew curtly, not looking up, fixing the last balsa frame into place.

The boy dropped the logs he was carrying.

"Watch out," said Andrew. "You nearly smashed my equipment. You could have looked."

Without so much as a glance at Andrew, the boy grabbed the model with both hands.

"Keep your hands off," said Andrew.

"I won't break it," said the boy eagerly.

Andrew watched as the boy ran his hands over every inch of the model, his agile fingers flickering back and forth.

"This tack won't hold. It's in crooked." And with a deft movement the boy pulled the tack out. "See!"

"You've got a nerve, coming in here unasked and smashing up my model."

Andrew was angry. He glared at the brown face and long, dark hair. But the boy was right. The tack wouldn't have held, and if he'd started building on it, it might have meant a lot of work wasted.

"Don't tell me, I'm guessing ... " said the boy, his fingers feeling along the balsa outline of the farm buildings. "It's going to be the farm, isn't it?"

How could the boy tell? Andrew only had the outline down. It didn't look like anything at all yet.

"Come on, you rascal," boomed a deep voice at the door. "Leave yer old grandad to do all the work. Ought to be ashamed of yourself."

"He's making a model, Gramps, of the farmyard."

The old man had a grizzled, bushy beard. Andrew couldn't see much of his face except for sunburnt cheeks under shaggy white eyebrows.

"Model, is it? I'll believe it when it's done. Now pick up those logs afore I skin you alive."

The boy laughed. He bent to pick up the logs, revealing strong, brown knees which poked out of grimy trousers. Instead he picked up the box of enamel paints, but before Andrew could complain, he set it quickly back on the floor.

"Where did I put the logs, Gramps?"

"On the right of that box, you varmint," called the old man. "Keep your mind on the job, boy."

"I've only been here a minute, Gramps."

"Well, if I don't skin you, you lazy so and so, you can bet your best boots Miss Beatrice will. How did you get in here then?"

"I heard him hammering the tacks in." The boy gathered up the logs and grinned at Andrew. "See you," he said. "Take care with those tacks."

"I've got my arms full," said the old man, "so the lovely young lady will guide you out. Go on now," he said to Bella, "he doesn't bite. Take his arm."

Bella looked in astonishment at Andrew. She reached up and held the boy's arm and together they walked to the door.

"Don't you believe Gramps. I'm a vampire and I bite," barked the boy. Bella shrieked with excitement.

Andrew stared at his base. In his mind he could still see the fingers flickering as delicately as butterflies over the balsa framework. "See you," he yelled suddenly at the open door.

Bella came running back up to Andrew. "He's funny. I like him, don't you?"

"Yes," said Andrew. "I think he's blind."

"Beatrice says to come. It's lunchtime," Joanna was standing at the door.

"Where have you been?" said Andrew.

Joanna shrugged her shoulders.

"If you've been exploring you might have told me."

"Come and see what Andrew is making," said Bella. "It's a model and this boy Simeon says it's going to be the farm." Bella dragged Joanna to the table.

"It's going to look just like the farm," explained Andrew, "and have a farmyard. Do you think I could sell it, Joanna? Would anyone want to buy a model of a real farmyard?"

Joanna barely glanced at the base. She never had the patience to make things like that herself, but usually she loved looking at Andrew's models and was eager with crazy suggestions. "I wouldn't know."

She walked away to the door.

"And you don't care either," shouted Andrew, angrily hiding the hurt.

· Chapter Five ·

They ate lunch in silence. It was a thick stew, packed with tender chunks of lamb. In the bowls on the table potatoes glistened in butter and fresh peas from the garden smelled of mint. With the meal came a crusty loaf that Beatrice must have baked that morning. Andrew hadn't expected her to be such a good cook and he tucked in hungrily after his breakfast of dry toast.

His plate half-empty, he noticed that Joanna had hardly touched her food. She sat there picking it over and spreading it around her plate. Something was definitely wrong with her. Joanna loved good food and she and Andrew often squabbled over shares. It had to be homesickness, but he would never have expected it of her.

Poor Bella had finished but she sat there glancing from face to face, with an expression of misery.

Beatrice moved from stove to table, limping and silent.

"Come and see my plans," said Andrew to Joanna as they finished the last of the washing-up and hung the wet drying-up cloths over the brass bar in front of the range. He felt sure he could find out what was wrong if only they could have a chat alone together. "I don't know what to do about the windows. I'm sure I could put in real glass . . ."

Joanna didn't stay to listen. She went towards the staircase and disappeared upstairs. Above them her bedroom door shut quietly. Beatrice smiled as she stacked the dishes.

Andrew slipped out, across the searing midday heat of the yard and into the barn. Its coolness enveloped him and soothed him. He was as much hurt by Joanna's attitude as angry with her. He'd keep himself to himself in future. No one was going to believe he'd spent the summer in the country. After a few more weeks in the barn, he'd be as white and pasty-faced as if he'd had a holiday in prison.

With care he measured the wall segments and began to cut them out with his hacksaw.

What should he do about Joanna? He wanted to write and tell Mum, but he couldn't worry her with any more. Anyway, what could he say? "Joanna's behaving strangely." It was hardly a life-threatening illness. And Dad had said he would cope. He had to. He'd put up with it.

The days that followed settled into the same pattern. Apart from his chores, Andrew kept well away from Beatrice, and busied himself in the barn with his model. The sun was becoming hotter each day, and as he burnt easily, Andrew convinced himself he was happier pottering in the barn.

He had been expecting and hoping that he would be sent back to Mum, but the dead hens were never mentioned again. The carcasses disappeared, so that he didn't have to clean or pluck them. He'd have refused to do it anyway.

Joanna stayed in her room in the heat of the day, but otherwise went out alone in the morning and again in the late afternoon. Andrew told himself he didn't care, but he knew he did. What made him feel more isolated was that Bella rarely came to see him in the barn. She seemed to be spending more and more time with Beatrice.

Progress on the model was slow but it didn't matter. He had till the end of the holidays and he didn't want to finish it too soon. It was the most ambitious model he had attempted.

Later in the week he sat pondering the problem of the windows. Joanna had rushed alone past the barn door and into the orchard. Later, Beatrice and Bella had ambled past hand in hand. Andrew felt miserable, caught in some dark underground cell while the sunlit life outside flowed to and fro without him. He checked the measurement of the window gap.

"Psst!"

Someone was in the corner. In the dim light Andrew could only make out a shadowy figure. Then the figure moved forward into the beam of sunlight streaming through the broken roof and Andrew glimpsed a toe poking out of an old trainer.

"It's me – Simeon."

"I can see that."

Simeon felt round the edge of the table. "I could see it was you too, a mile off."

"You couldn't . . . I mean you're . . ."

"You're wrong. I've got X-ray vision."

Andrew listened, interested.

"I can see in the dark. It's the cosmic molecules. They feed in sight through the top of my head. It's a rare gift."

"OK. What colour is my hair? It's dark enough in here for cosmic molecules."

Simeon stretched out his hands towards Andrew. He waved them around and moaned to himself. Andrew watched suspiciously.

"Hot . . . hot, like lava from a volcano. That's red, isn't it?"

"You're wrong. My hair is a sort of sandy brown. I don't believe you."

Simeon sidled round the table. "Stand up, let me feel."

Andrew stood opposite the boy. Simeon's hands stroked his hair and then his fingers ran round his face, following the contours of his eyebrows, nose, mouth and chin. His fingers were as light and ticklish as a feather. "Terrible!" he declared. "I feel sorry for you."

"Why?" Did Simeon have special powers? Could Simeon see how utterly miserable he was?

"You're so ugly. You're a toad."

Andrew stuck his foot out without thinking so that it caught behind Simeon's calf. It worked with Ben every time. Simeon tried to step back but instead fell over Andrew's foot, but he pulled Andrew down with him. They rolled in the dust, pummelling and groaning as dramatically as the Saturday wrestling on TV.

Simeon got Andrew into a sort of armlock, but Andrew tugged on Simeon's shirt. There was a sharp rip. They both stopped and sat up.

"Was that your shirt?" said Andrew.

"It's all right," said Simeon. "Lets the air in – good ventilation. What are you doing about the windows?"

They both staggered to their feet. So Simeon must have been there examining the model before Andrew came in.

"I haven't decided."

"I've made hundreds, thousands of models."

Andrew didn't believe Simeon, but he didn't want him to go. "You can help me, if you like," he said carelessly. "But it's not for keeping. I'm going to sell it."

"I might. Are we sharing? The money I mean."

"I know it's not fair, and I'll understand if you don't want to help, but Dad's desperate. He's got to have the money."

"Move over then. You're not having all the bench to yourself."

They were busy most of the morning. Simeon held the wood steady while Andrew sawed. Simeon was better at gluing and assembling the fiddly joints than Andrew. His fingers felt the tiniest inaccuracy and he was never satisfied until a joint was perfectly aligned.

By lunchtime all the walls were in place with the windows cut out.

A shadow fell across the doorway. It was a while before Andrew realised what it was. He jerked back to see a thin shape leaning on a stick. The shape moved away as he turned, and Beatrice's voice faded into the courtyard.

"Lunch. I shan't call again."

"I wonder how long she's been there," said Andrew. "She can't have seen you, thank goodness. She hates men."

"I know that," said Simeon. "You go and I'll slip away after you've gone."

"Can you . . .? I mean, can you see your way alone?"

"Course I can. How do you think I got in? I know every part round here."

"But when you brought the logs . . ."

"I hadn't been in here before, but if I go once and have Gramps close by, I don't forget."

Joanna walked into the yard.

"Where have you been, Joanna?" Andrew yelled as he ran out after her into the sunshine.

Joanna walked into the house without a backward glance.

The next morning, for the first time since they arrived, Andrew woke up pleased at the prospect of the day. Simeon might already be in the barn. They were going to work out how to make the yard fence and gates. He caught himself smiling as he cleaned his teeth. He mustn't do that. Beatrice might get suspicious and it would be awful if she stopped Simeon from coming.

In the kitchen, the sun streamed in through the windows. Bella was chattering to Beatrice and Beatrice was smiling. She looked a different woman when she smiled.

Andrew tried to look convincingly sullen. Beatrice ignored him, but she poured a cup of tea from the big brown pot and pushed it over the table towards him. Andrew was surprised. She usually left him to serve himself with everything. If he hadn't, he'd have starved days ago.

"No Joanna?" said Beatrice to Bella. "She's sleeping late this morning. It's all this walking she does. The girl must be tired out. Still, it's unlike her not to be up neat and tidy for breakfast."

It was meant for him, Andrew knew, but Beatrice wouldn't talk to him directly.

"I'll go and look," said Andrew.

He wasn't doing it to save Beatrice the trouble, he told himself, he needed to check on Joanna before he went to the barn.

Andrew hadn't been in Joanna's bedroom since that first night. The room was empty and the bed unmade, but there was no mess. It didn't look like the friendly muddle of Joanna's room at home. Apart from the slept-in bed, you wouldn't believe anyone was living there. Joanna's suitcase lay on the floor. Andrew kicked it open. It hadn't been unpacked.

"She's not in her room," said Andrew as he rushed back into the kitchen.

"Joanna?" said Bella suddenly interested. "She tiptoed past my door, but I was playing with Beagles and I heard her."

"You heard her?" said Beatrice. "Why didn't you tell me, dear?"

Bella looked coy. Andrew knew why she hadn't told: she hadn't thought it important and she was so much enjoying being Beatrice's pet that she didn't want Joanna coming in to share it.

"Why didn't you tell *me*?" said Andrew fiercely.

"Why should I?" said Bella, her voice faltering. "Don't look at me like that, Andrew. It's not my fault."

"Where could she have gone?" said Andrew.

"Beagles and I spied on her from our window. She goes up to the woods. She's always going there."

"Of course that's all right, Bella," soothed Beatrice. "She'll be back when she wants her breakfast."

Bella beamed.

Andrew was furious. If *he* didn't bother to turn up for breakfast he was sure Beatrice would create another unholy scene. It was all right for the girls. *They* could get away with murder.

He shovelled in his sausages and egg and gulped down his tea. The toast he left untouched. Seeing Beatrice look at it, Andrew thought for a moment that she was going to speak to him, but she turned away to the sink.

He was uneasy about Joanna. Usually she lay in in the holidays, until Mum nagged her out of bed, and she never went without breakfast. Blow it! She was ruining everything. What if Simeon came to help on the model and found Andrew was out? He might not bother to come again. But Andrew couldn't get down to work not knowing where Joanna was, not in the odd mood she was in.

In the sunlit yard Andrew immediately felt more cheerful. He checked the barn but there was no sign of Simeon. The cracks in the mud were widening into ruts and the soft sogginess beneath was hardening. The sky was an expanse of blue and the heat of the sun promised yet another hot day. He was letting Joanna get him down. He really shouldn't worry so much about her. After all, he had chosen to shut himself away in the barn for days, so he hadn't been much company either.

He went through the old orchard to the gate at the far side. It was strange to think he had never bothered to look over, let alone explore. He climbed to the top of the gate, lay flat on his tummy, and vaulted over. The neighbouring field was sown with wheat, now turning to gold. The heads of corn were beginning to bend slightly with the weight of the ripening grain.

"Joanna!" Andrew bellowed.

He stood still. There was no reply. In the distance he could hear a dull hammering. A quick snuffling caught up with him from behind. Sam bounded up, tail wagging joyfully. "Not you, Sam. I want Joanna."

He ran round the field, listening to the faint rattle of the corn that he disturbed at the field's edge. Tentacles of bramble scratched his legs, but the long grass had been worn down into something resembling a path. At the far side he came to another gate. He climbed it and gazed out at a field of cropped grass with a haystack in the corner, protected by a beaten-up iron roof on rusty iron legs. Beyond the field, open heath led up the hill to the wood at the top.

The hammering sounded nearer.

"Joanna!"

The hammering stopped and then started again. Sam whined.

"Sam, you are a nuisance. I'll have to open the gate for you."

Sam patiently sat wagging his tail as Andrew untied the old rope on the gate. He bounded through and then charged back and forth over the field, his nose glued to the ground. Andrew knew how Sam felt. He couldn't think why he had sat for days in the gloom of the barn.

The morning sunlight had yet to become harsh with the midday heat. It warmed Andrew's back as he stood staring at the ripening corn, dotted with crimson from clumps of poppies. Andrew threw back his head, wallowing in the vast blueness overhead. There was so much space after the barn. He felt like a prisoner released. This was how he had imagined the countryside would be. This was what he had looked forward to. No wonder Joanna liked escaping out here alone. There was no mystery to it. He'd got things horribly out of proportion shut away in that barn.

But now he was here he might as well find her, and she was sure to be in a better mood away from the farm.

Andrew followed Sam through a narrow cutting in the hedge on to the heath. Small blue butterflies danced above the grass ahead of him, but further still, on the edge of the wood, he saw two figures, one crouching and the other swinging something heavy. A distant whistle from the larger figure and Sam raced up towards him barking with delight.

It was Simeon's grandfather. Sam raced round and round him as Gramps pretended to catch him. Simeon sat on the ground laughing.

Andrew ran up the heath track. It was all working out!

Here was Simeon and it was a wonderful day and all the heath was waiting to be explored.

"Simeon!" Andrew yelled. "I thought you were coming to help me with the model."

Gramps laid down his heavy mallet and wiped his forehead with the back of a faded sleeve.

"It's all right for some folks, but Simeon and me, we've got to make a livin' if we're goin' to eat."

"What are you doing?" asked Andrew curiously.

"Splittin' logs." Simeon held up a large wedge of tapered iron. "I hold this steady on the log, then Gramps hammers it and we split the log. Then the pieces will fit in a fireplace or stove."

"Champion day it is," said Gramps, sinking down on the fallen tree trunk they had been cutting up. "How's it goin' then?"

"What going?"

"Beatrice like. Never known her let a boy or man into the house afore."

Andrew looked at Gramps. His eyes were lost behind the shaggy white eyebrows but his mouth was set in a firm line. The big ears and face that emerged from the crescent of grizzled beard were as tanned and ruddy as the brown boots on his feet. It was a stern but kindly face and it brought back to Andrew how alone and friendless he had felt in the last few days.

"Not too well. We had a bit of a fight. I shouldn't have, but she won't believe me. She thinks I'm a liar. Now she pretends I'm not there."

"She's not all bad, boy. We's known each other since we were children – went to school together. She was a bit of a sweetheart at one time, as you might say, but it weren't no good – she was too scared."

Beatrice scared?

"Her mother died when she was about the age of that young sister of yours. Used to come with me to school some days with bruises on her arms and then it got so bad, some days her face was blue."

"What do you mean?"

" 'Twas was that brute of a father. Always wanted a son to take over the farm, but he only got one child. Tried to turn Beatrice into the boy he never had, only he treat her worse. When her mother died, there were no one to protect her. But she was never good enough for him. The least thing wrong and he hit her."

Andrew remembered the hands in front of Beatrice's face, the terrified look on her face. Beatrice *had* been scared. Had she really expected Andrew to hit her with the whip?

Gramps rested his chin on the long handle of his mallet, as if happy to take a break.

"When I became a lad she weren't allowed to walk to school with me any more. But I used to spy on her. One day I saw him hit her in the yard with a crop. She'd turned over a milk churn, she was that nervous. Well, that was it. I went in and knocked him clean down."

Gramps' deep chuckle emerged more like a growl. He pulled a rag from his pocket, wiped his forehead, and then stuffed the handkerchief back.

"He chased me but I was a quick lad and got away. Poor Beatrice, we didn't see her for weeks. He told the school she had the measles but there weren't a child ill with measles for miles around."

Gramps stared out over the heath as if he had forgotten Andrew and Simeon, as if he were concentrating to remember.

"One day I'm going to school and she's waiting and she tells me never to come near her again, that I were as bad as her father, that all men thought they could hit and fight their way through life, and the world 'ud be a lot better if the ground opened and swallowed the lot of them."

Andrew listened, amazed. His mother couldn't have known all this. "Couldn't you persuade her to change her mind?"

Gramps chuckled, hauled himself up off the log and picked up his mallet.

"No lad stays where he's not wanted. I found a better sweetheart: Simeon's gran. A true Romany she was, and she gave up travellin' to marry me. Made me the best wife I could have, and in heaven for sure now. But look what she left me – this rascal of a grandson." Gramps nudged Simeon with his mallet.

"Get on, you lazy so and so. Pick up that wedge. Mind you, I always kept a soft spot for Beatrice, and I'm the only man she allows on the farm to help out. Couldn't believe it when I heard you were there, so we came to look for ourselves, didn't we, Simeon?"

Simeon grinned and nodded. "I'll come this afternoon

and we'll do the windows," he offered. "I've got to help Gramps with this tree first."

"I've got to find Joanna. You haven't seen her, my older sister? She's got brown, curly hair . . ."

Simeon laughed.

"Oh, I'm sorry, Simeon. I mean . . . I've been looking for her."

"I haven't heard her," Simeon said. "At least she hasn't come past since we've been here."

"Where's Sam? He was here a minute ago. Joanna! Sam!" Andrew shouted.

All three stood still, listening to the soft answering coo of the wood pigeons.

"Joanna!"

Simeon sank to his knees by the tack and moved his hands flat over the grass. "Sam's gone up to the woods. The grass has been trodden on." Simeon's hands flickered over the grass. "Someone else has been here since the dew fell. They've pressed the grass flat with their feet so that the sun's dried it. The tall grass is still damp. Not big feet mind, not a man's feet."

"It must be Joanna!" cried Andrew. "Bella said she saw her. She says she's always going up here. You'd think she'd stay out of the woods in the sunny weather, but she's always going off on her own. She's got mean and . . . and . . . sort of empty." It was a relief to tell someone at last.

Gramps raised the mallet above his head as he listened, then he hesitated and laid it back down. Andrew was pleased Gramps didn't laugh at him. Gramps stared at the woods, then at the fields of ripe corn below him and scratched his beard.

"The sun . . . A lass should be out in the sunshine after all the rain we've had. I don't remember a worse summer, till you all came. Thought the harvest was surely lost. Never known a summer like it."

Andrew felt a pang of disappointment. Gramps wasn't interested, and why should he be? He didn't know Joanna. He was rambling on like an old man.

"I'm going to look in the woods then."

"Hold on!" said Gramps. "You take Simeon."

Andrew looked at Simeon doubtfully. It wasn't a game. If he had to lead Simeon everywhere it would slow him. Joanna would hear them coming. She was so odd now, she might even run away.

"Take him," said Gramps. "He knows the woods like the back of his hand."

And he did.

Simeon took Andrew by the elbow and led him into the shade beneath the beech trees. His other hand he held outstretched in front of him, wary of low branches.

After the merciless sunshine on the heath, the air beneath the canopy of trees was cool and refreshing. Underfoot the ground was soft and deep with old leaves and beech mast, but here and there, where a ray of sunlight had broken through the overhead branches, a patch of emerald grass sprouted.

"Do you really come here often?" whispered Andrew.

He wasn't sure why he was whispering. The beech mast underfoot deadened the sound of their steps, but now that he was so close to Joanna, Andrew was curious. He didn't want her knowing he was there.

"I used to come here all the time, except before the harvest. Gran brought me when I was a kid – showed me all over."

"Your gran?"

"She's dead now. But she raised me when my mother went travelling. She said travelling was no life for a child that'd never see."

"Travelling?"

"Yeah. My gran was a Romany. She gave up travelling for Gramps, but my mum has the Romany blood. She has to travel."

"You mean she left you?"

Simeon pulled a branch back, brushed past it and then held it back for Andrew.

"That's how it looks to you. But there's all ways. She comes round and it's like – a holiday, but she'd never be happy if she stopped travelling."

"Why doesn't she take you?"

"Gran was right. I need to know a place, so that I can get around alone. How would you like it if you were led all your life like some dog on a lead? I know the fields and heath round here better than Miss Beatrice who owns them, and it makes no difference, day or night, I know my way. With my mum I'd be stuck in a caravan, always travelling, afraid to go out."

"But your mother . . . Does she miss you?"

"Does your mother miss you?"

"Yes," sighed Andrew, remembering his mother's face as she got into the car.

"It's a daft question then, isn't it?"

The beeches had given way to dank yew trees. A solid belt of towering, interlocking yews with massive black trunks blocked their way.

"Look at those," said Andrew. "Those trunks . . . They must be hundreds of years old."

The branches of the yews hung low, smothered with dark green needles. They forced Andrew to crouch and duck as he followed Simeon. The ground beneath the yews was wet and squelchy, as if the sun never penetrated the dense branches. As they pushed their way through, mosquitoes rose from the branches and swarms of gnats circled their heads.

The silence was suffocating. Even the distant birdsong among the beeches was stifled by the evergreen wall.

"Did I not tell you?" Simeon turned back to Andrew. "This place is haunted."

Andrew stared at Simeon. Simeon was talking rot again, although it was difficult to be sure. His brown eyes gave nothing away. Simeon's mouth quivered.

"Oh yes," said Andrew. "So that's why you're always up here?"

"You weren't half afraid."

"No – I wasn't."

"You stopped breathing. I heard."

Andrew laughed. "How many ghosts have you heard here then?"

"It wasn't me. It was my gran. She said never in summer to come further than the beeches, till the harvest was in —"

"Or the ghouls would get you! Do they vanish after the harvest? Simeon, where are you?"

The branches were too dense to allow Andrew to grip Simeon's arm. He had slipped away, disappeared among the dark blanket of yew leaves.

"Simeon!"

"An . . . dr . . . ew . . ." whispered a voice behind him.

Andrew spun round and bumped his head on an overhanging branch. The air was still and heavy and the ground gave off a damp, rotting smell. He lurched forward. "You're a lousy ghoul," he said angrily, rubbing his head. "You didn't fool me."

"I did."

"Didn't."

"Why'd you fall over then?" Simeon suddenly stretched out his hand. "Listen!"

Simeon strained forward through the branches. Andrew couldn't hear a thing, but he followed Simeon, pushing the wet branches aside.

They emerged on a narrow path, overgrown and unused. Then Andrew heard it: a high-pitched wailing.

Simeon's face was taut with the effort of listening. "I told you – ghouls," he said uncertainly.

"What do you mean?"

But the path had come to an end. Round a corner it

unexpectedly opened out on to a treeless plateau. Andrew saw that this circular clearing, surrounded by a wall of towering yew trees, must be the hilltop. Edged back against a yew trunk sat Sam, his ears pinned back, whining and howling. Along his back a ridge of hairs stood darkly upright. In the centre of the circle stood Joanna, preoccupied and still, staring at the turf beneath her.

"Joanna!" Andrew called.

He shivered. The towering curtain of yews shut out the early morning sun, so that most of the clearing was in shade, gloomy and chill.

Simeon held out a hand to push him back. "Keep back, Andrew, and look at the turf. Sam – he's not gone in."

In his excitement at finding Joanna, Andrew hadn't noticed the turf. It was cut into intricate and winding paths, barely wide enough to get one foot on. To either side of the turf paths the grass had been cut away to expose the white chalk of the hill beneath.

"It's like a maze," he said in astonishment.

Then he saw that there were several entrances of turf path leading into the maze and that, although they wound back and forth in patterns too complicated to disentangle, they all seemed to lead to the far side of the clearing. There, a square platform of turf, wide enough to hold several men, lay against the furthest yew trees.

It reminded Andrew of those puzzles you got in books for rainy days, where you had to find your way through a maze with a pencil to get the rabbit back home.

And there, halfway in, stood the rabbit.

Joanna appeared not to notice them. Her hands fingered the locket at her neck as she stared with a puzzled look at the turf she was standing on. Not even Sam's whining could distract her. She moved forward along a path, came to a dead end, retraced her footsteps, pondered again and then set off along a different path.

Sam leapt off his haunches and growled and whined.

Simeon's hand pressed on Andrew's arm. "What's she doing? Tell me. What's Sam up to?"

"She's . . . she's in a sort of maze."

"I know that. I've been here often enough before."

"I think she's trying to find her way to a sort of square area of grass on the far side."

Simeon's hand fell to Sam's ears and the upright bristles on his back. Sam edged away, never taking his eyes off Joanna.

"Listen to Sam. He knows. We've got to get her out."

Andrew wasn't sure why, but he knew too they had to get her out. "Why have we got to?"

"I promised my gran never to go into the maze until after the harvest was in. I wouldn't have come, but Gramps sent me with you. He must have guessed you'd need help."

Andrew thought back to when he had told Gramps about Joanna. Perhaps he had got it wrong and Gramps had taken notice after all.

Andrew watched as Joanna inched slowly forward, occasionally moving on to a dead end, but patiently wending her way back and trying again. Sam was becoming more and more agitated, now leaping at the edge of the maze and barking.

They must get Joanna.

Andrew chose a path, but was yanked back by Simeon. "You follow me," said Simeon. "I've done it before. There's not much time."

Simeon stepped forward slowly but surely, feeling the turf in front with the tip of his battered trainers. Joanna was moving closer to the grass square, but Simeon was gaining ground rapidly.

Backwards and forwards wound the path Simeon followed, sometimes appearing so close to the platform of turf that Andrew was sure they had discovered the route across. But then it led back as far as the outer edge again. Just when they seemed furthest away from Joanna the path led directly in, round a corner and they were by her side.

Andrew leant forward and grabbed her.

"What are you doing, Joanna?" said Andrew.

For a moment Andrew felt ridiculous. Had he and Simeon just worked themselves up into a state about the ghouls and the haunted nonsense? Good thing Dad wasn't here to laugh at him. Why shouldn't he put his foot down on to the chalk and run straight back to the edge with Joanna? He lifted his foot, but he found he was too frightened to put it down. Sam watched him and howled. He drew his foot back and took Joanna's other hand.

She didn't seem to mind and allowed Andrew to lead her back, in and out of the waves of turf track till they reached the edge.

Sam went wild, leaping up at Joanna, licking her.

"What do you do up here every day?"

The sunlight flashed on her locket and she was gone.

Andrew stared after her, stunned, then he and Sam raced after her along the path through the yew trees to where it stretched down the hill into the distance. Below him, he saw Joanna running down to where the road lay.

So this was the path Joanna had brought Bella up to have a wee. Andrew could see the exact spot where the car had been parked and he had tied up the silencer. Simeon and he had joined the path higher up, near the top, after working up through the wood from the heath on the far side.

"Andrew!" Far behind him Simeon's call echoed.

He'd never catch Joanna now. She was probably going back to the farm for lunch anyway. Andrew raced back up the path to the yews.

"Where'd you go so sudden?" said Simeon crossly.

"She ran off. I had to try and catch her, but she went too quickly."

"And you let her go – after we got her out."

"I couldn't stop her. It's all so odd. I'm not sure what to think. Did we have to get her out?"

"I reckon so."

"But I didn't see anything. She was just mucking around in that maze, wasn't she?"

"I felt it and so did Sam."

"What did you feel?"

Simeon scratched his head. "I don't know, but I reckon my gran was right."

· Chapter Six ·

Simeon didn't come that afternoon. Andrew started gluing the floor sections into the farmhouse frame. It was fiddly work and he missed Simeon, but he had sneaked out a box of matches from the kitchen and found he could get the glue on better with the matchstick end.

"Didn't you hear me calling? Beatrice has got tea on the table. We've got a lemon cake. I helped her make it." Bella stood at the barn door. She didn't bother to come in any more to see what Andrew was doing. She hung around Beatrice instead, and sometimes Andrew could hear their laughter and chatter when the kitchen door was open.

He was disappointed that Simeon hadn't come. Simeon was the one person who made this place bearable.

"The lemon cake has worked well, Bella," said Beatrice.

She cut Andrew a slice and slid it across the kitchen table without a word.

"Where's Joanna?"

"She's had her tea and gone out. There's nothing like the evening after a hot day. Shall we have a walk before bed, Bella?"

"I'll come," said Andrew slowly.

Beatrice looked at him for the first time. "The chores," she said sharply, "are they done? And you're to light the range so we have hot water tonight. I let it go out. It heats the kitchen to an inferno in this weather."

Andrew wanted to say, "It can wait", but there'd be no hot water for baths or washing if he left it. He'd better do it.

He fed the range with coal from the scuttle and kindling from the basket. He scrunched up an old newspaper and added a firelighter.

"Where are the matches?" As soon as he'd said it, he remembered. "They're in the barn. I borrowed them."

Beatrice was washing up at the sink.

"You borrowed them without asking?" she said. "You took them to please yourself. How were we to light the stove if you hadn't been here?"

"I'm sorry. I meant to bring them back. I'll go and get them."

As Andrew ran across the yard, he thought how Beatrice was the sort of person who could twist the slightest forgetfulness into some wicked wrongdoing. There were people like that, who, whatever you did, always read the worst into it. Joanna – that was what was so good about Joanna – and Dad – they believed the best of everybody and somehow they got the best. Or rather that was how Joanna had been.

The matches weren't on the table in the barn. Andrew searched hard. It was unlike him to lose things; he was a careful and organised worker. With Bella calling him he'd hurried in and forgotten the matches and now he couldn't remember where he'd left them. He was sure he had left them on the table.

"I can't find them."

"You can't find them!" exploded Beatrice. "You take them without asking, carelessly lose them – how are we to light the range?"

"Can't we sort of rub some sticks together?" whispered Bella anxiously. "They did that, you know, cavemen."

"You will walk to the village tomorrow and buy some more. Tonight we will have to wash in cold water, thanks to your selfishness."

Beatrice banged the crockery about in the last of the tepid water. Andrew picked up a tea towel and started wiping the plates.

The window above the sink was misting up so Beatrice leant forward to unlatch it, but she remained bent, peering through the window.

Over her shoulder Andrew glimpsed a figure flash by across the yard and into the barn. It was Simeon.

"I've seen that boy hanging round here before. I'll not have it. Tell him to go," Beatrice said icily.

Andrew went out to the barn and found Simeon sitting in front of the model.

"You've got the floors in – it's great. I think they'll hold . . . "

The sight of Simeon sitting in front of the model was the most welcome bit of the day. If only Beatrice hadn't seen him.

"You've got to go," Andrew sighed. "She saw you come in."

"I couldn't get here earlier. Look what I found on the path. You should look after these." Simeon held out the box of matches. It was squashed and broken. "I stood on it. They were just by the gate. You shouldn't carry them around in your pocket."

Andrew took the box and pushed it back into shape. Most of the matches had fallen out but a few remained.

"Can you come tomorrow?" he asked. "We could put on the roof. Maybe we could get it ready to take into town, try it out at a toyshop."

"Tomorrow? Can you finish painting it? That'll be great. How much shall we ask for it? Five hundred pounds? Six hundred?"

Andrew laughed. "Fifteen pounds if we're lucky! Maybe nobody will want it."

Andrew took the matches back into the kitchen and lit the stove. He left the box on the mantelpiece where it always lived. Beatrice would see it there.

Then he saw the letter, sitting on the mantelpiece, the address in his mother's handwriting. Andrew snatched it down. The envelope had been opened. It was a letter to all three of them and Joanna had already read it, but no one had told him about it. In the old days Joanna would have run out to him in the barn, yelling and laughing, and they would have opened the letter together and read it to Bella too.

Andrew clutched the letter, his knuckles white. There in the envelope was Mum, the normal world, the real world, and here he was living in a hostile world from which he was excluded, and where everything had been turned upside-down.

"... give Bella a big hug for me and say I miss her as much as she misses me. Joanna, don't be too noisy and rowdy. Remember Beatrice isn't young and is not used to pop-music-mad teenage girls, and, Andrew, I'm sure you're having a wonderful time exploring the country – isn't it just the holiday you've always wanted?"

Everything was wrong. Bella was loving every minute with Beatrice now. Joanna slipped in and out like some silent and insubstantial shadow. As for himself, it was his worst holiday ever. Mum couldn't have dreamt what it would be like.

"Dad hasn't found a job and it's costing him to live, so it's worrying. The restaurant is all right. I'm saving the tips and then I'll get a coach down to see you all. Andrew – the silencer held but it cost too much to replace, so I decided to sell the car. I'm too busy to use it and when I'm free I just like to stay in, I'm that tired. The restaurant is closed on Monday. The next free one I have I'll come and visit. Be good, Bella! Keep smiling, Joanna, and turn down that music, and, Andrew, plan a nice walk for me when I come ..."

Where was Joanna? Andrew rushed into the yard, across the orchard and into the wheatfield. "Joanna!" he yelled. "Joanna!"

There was no sign of her and no answer. In the distance a plume of smoke revealed where Simeon and his grandfather must still be burning kindling from the tree they had felled. The sky was already darkening in the east and the remaining sun's rays were low and golden.

Bella wandered round the corner of the field, jumping over the bramble shoots as she held Beatrice's hand.

"When will they cut the corn, Beatrice?" Andrew heard her high child's voice.

Beatrice followed, holding in one hand a bunch of red poppies they had picked together.

"If this sun keeps up, we'll be able to start in two or three days. Peter is coming round tomorrow to check out the combine harvester."

"Can I ride in it?"

"There's only one seat, and Peter drives it alone."

Hand in hand the little girl and the old woman meandered through the trees and back into the yard.

Andrew stared after them. He had been afraid he'd be landed with looking after Bella, but now he scarcely saw anything of her. He missed her getting in the way and climbing all over him and asking him to swing her. Dad had asked him to look after the girls but he wasn't needed, and no one was interested in him.

He watched Beatrice and Bella open the gate into the orchard. Unnoticed, he followed them, shooed the four remaining hens into the pen and latched the gate. On the way back he checked in the barn. It was almost too dark to see much but he tidied up the table and set out his paints ready for the morning.

As he climbed the stairs from the kitchen he heard Bella splashing in the bath, talking to Beatrice. The water must be hot now. Beatrice might have mentioned it or even thanked him for lighting the range.

On the landing outside Joanna's door, he hesitated. Beatrice was in the bathroom with Bella and would be there for a while. Andrew turned the door handle. The room was in shadow now that the evening sun had moved to the far side of the farm, but outlined in the window, sitting on the window seat, was Joanna.

"Joanna! I didn't know you were here. You must have heard me calling outside."

Joanna's head turned, a dark outline against the golden light outside.

"Why didn't you tell me Mum had written?"

Joanna turned back to look out of the window.

"Poor Mum. It sounds bad. Dad's not got any work, and she's had to sell the car. I hope she's not having to work too hard. At least she doesn't have to look after . . . "

Joanna sat motionless.

"I've had enough!" said Andrew, fighting back the tears that welled up uncontrollably. "You could at least listen to me. If Mum and Dad didn't have so much to worry about I'd tell them. Oh, what's the use. You're a selfish pig!"

The old Joanna would have risen in fury at that, but this stranger sat still, ignoring Andrew. That was the worst thing; being ignored by Beatrice was bad enough, but it was far, far worse to be ignored by Joanna. He had had about all he could take . . .

He stormed up behind her and jerked her face round. He would force her to look at him, to notice him. "I hate you!" he whispered with all the loathing he could muster.

Close to, Joanna's brown eyes were as vacant and expressionless as Simeon's, but if Simeon's eyes were dead every other bit of him was alive and alert. Joanna seemed dead everywhere, apart from the mechanical movements that indicated otherwise. She turned away and stared through the open window, the locket round her neck shimmering in a golden glow and her pale face bathed in an unfamiliar rosy light. What was it?

The dusk had deepened into a uniform grey, but leaping and dancing up into the charcoal sky were tongues of yellow, orange and red. There was a distant crackling and popping and a spray of sparks shot as high as an exploding firework. A fire!

"Where is it?" Andrew shouted.

Not in the orchard but beyond the wheatfield, not far enough for the woods, so not a woodcutter's fire.

Andrew burst into the bathroom. "Beatrice!" He grabbed her by the arm.

The old woman pulled away in panic, but Andrew wouldn't let her go. He dragged her into Joanna's room and pointed out of the window.

"The haystack!" Beatrice cried.

"I'll call the fire brigade," shouted Andrew as he leapt downstairs.

As he dialled 999, Beatrice hobbled into the kitchen. "Pitchforks – in the barn. The fire engine will take too long. We must get the burning hay off or we lose all this year's hay."

Outside it was dark now, although as Andrew hauled the ladder through the orchard, the trees danced to life in the flickering from the distant fire. The ladder was very heavy. Beatrice tried to carry one end, but she couldn't walk fast enough to keep up with Andrew. She held the gate open for him and Andrew struggled round the wheatfield, towards the orange glow leaping above the hedge. A smell of burning hung in the air and he could hear hissing and crackling as the flames fed on the dry hay.

As Andrew half-carried and half-dragged the ladder into the hayfield he saw the corrugated iron roof of the makeshift barn glowing red and collapsed sideways on buckled legs. One end of the stack was alight.

Beatrice set to with a rake, pulling the smouldering hay off the side. Andrew heaved the ladder against the other end, climbed up and crawled along the top of the stack. The heat was suffocating.

"The smoke!" Beatrice called. "Stay out of the smoke!"

With the pitchfork Andrew threw the burning hay over the side, clear of the stack. Steadily he moved forward and sideways, his arms taking on a life and will of their own. The hay on top was light and slid off easily, but the hay underneath was heavy and sodden and a sickening white smoke seeped out of it. The hot weather had dried the outside of the stack but inside it was still wet. He must get the burning hay off . . . Forward, dig in, throw . . .

The smoke was thick and choking. Andrew coughed and gasped for breath. Beatrice shouted beneath him and he staggered back, unable to stand the heat any longer. Somewhere, close to him, he could smell singeing hair. He made a grab at the ladder as a great billow of suffocating smoke rose from the wet hay. He was driven back, falling . . .

"Steady on," came a deep voice close at hand. "Here, Beatrice, you take his arm."

Gramps' gruff voice echoed in his ear. Andrew felt himself pulled to the ground and dragged back to the hedge. Gramps was puffing and Beatrice hobbled with the effort.

"You've done a grand job, lad. With any luck we'll save this end of the stack."

Andrew's eyes hurt, but he could just make out Gramps moving back to the rick with the rake. Beatrice took up the pitchfork beside him.

He couldn't leave the two old people on their own. Andrew staggered unsteadily to his feet. His legs didn't seem to want to do what they were told. He fell back and caught sight of Simeon, standing on the other side of the gate, his face lit up by a flare of flame. "Simeon ... " he tried to call. It came out as a croak. The flare subsided and the darkness swallowed Simeon up again.

"Was that Simeon?" Gramps called. "Don't let him in. I told him not to ... "

A siren shrieked over the crackling and hissing. An engine roared, got stuck and revved again. It must be in the orchard. Andrew heard shouts from the wheatfield that grew until the gate pillar gave way and the heavy fire engine swung into the hayfield.

With nothing left for him to do, Andrew gazed numbly as men in helmets ran round the barn, dragging hoses like sneaking snakes, until a spray of silver engulfed and doused the smoking stack. Then it was dark, apart from the light from the rising moon. The firemen stood ankle deep in mud and a tangle of hoses they were methodically rewinding.

"Beats me," said the leader of the crew. He took his helmet off and wiped his bald head and the back of his thick neck. Then he shook his head as he unbuttoned his black jacket, releasing a smell of drenching sweat. "It was only dry on the first six inches, still wet underneath. That's not the way a fire starts deep in hay, not unless it's been lit."

Andrew couldn't make out Beatrice's expression in the dark.

"We'll have to make a police report."

He saw Beatrice nod.

In the kitchen Bella was waiting in her pyjamas. "It was a big fire, wasn't it? I watched from my window. I wish I could have come. I heard the siren – it was scary and exciting, and the fire engine came right through the yard. You do look funny, you two, all dirty."

Beatrice's grey hair hung in wisps, and her high cheeks were smudged with soot and dirt. To her clothes hung strands of hay and cinders. She sank into a chair at the end of the table. "Time for bed, Bella," she said wearily. Bella kissed Beatrice obediently and pranced up the stairs.

Andrew stood there, exhausted. Surely Beatrice would talk to him and thank him now.

Her hands were clenched in front of her on the table. "I should never," she muttered, "never have let myself be persuaded." But it was a voice of despair and defeat.

She couldn't think . . . Surely she didn't?

Andrew walked up to Beatrice and looked down at the bent grey head. "You know I didn't do it. And if you think I did, you . . . you must be mad."

Beatrice raised her head and pointed at the mantelpiece. "You tell me then – who put the matches back?"

· CHAPTER SEVEN ·

"Wake up, Andrew. We're going into town. You've been asleep for ages."

Andrew opened his eyes as Bella climbed on to his bed and bounced around on his feet. It hurt.

"Get off, Bella! What's the time?"

"You've been asleep for ages and ages. We've had breakfast. Beatrice said we'd go without you, but I said it wasn't fair and . . ."

Andrew grabbed his watch and rubbed his eyes. Nearly ten o'clock. He'd been asleep for hours but he still felt exhausted.

It was two days since the fire. The previous day he had slept late too, and had spent the day avoiding Beatrice, working quietly in the barn, fitting the roof and painting the model farm.

He slid back into bed and pulled up the sheet.

"We're going into town," Bella said again as she shook his shoulder. "Don't you want to take the model to a toyshop?"

The farmyard . . . to a toyshop? Andrew sat up and reached for his clothes on the chair. "Tell Beatrice to wait. Give me half an hour. You try, Bella – she'll wait if you ask her."

Bella slid off the bed with a self-satisfied smile. "I'll ask her. She's ever so kind, Andrew. She won't mind if I ask her nicely."

Bella walked briskly to the door, full of importance for her task as messenger.

Andrew slipped into the barn. No sign of Simeon again. It was a shame the farmyard wasn't quite finished. He pulled out a small pot of black enamel paint, dipped his brush in and painted a round doorknob on the front door.

That looked better. Gingerly he lifted the base and carried the model out into the yard and over to the battered green car in which Beatrice, Joanna and Bella sat waiting.

"Look at that!" exclaimed Bella. "I wish it was for me."

In the sunlight the model took on a different quality. The silver paint of the gates and fences gleamed. The door from the house into the yard was painted blue, brilliant against the brick-red walls that Andrew had painstakingly marked out in grey, every brick. The barns had their full complement of slates painted in dark grey on their roofs, with no holes open to the sky, and for each barn there were wooden doors that opened and shut. On the older wing of the farm Andrew had painted the corner bricks and the cream-coloured plaster on the walls. The model was identical with the farm, apart from the older bit not having a thatched roof.

"It's just like the farm!" said Bella, peering over it delightedly. "But much newer and better, not so broken. Look, Joanna, it's the best thing Andrew has ever made."

Andrew was about to say, "But Simeon helped me",

when he remembered Beatrice. She was twisted round in the driving seat and staring at the farm on his knee, a look of astonishment on her face.

Joanna glanced over her shoulder and then looked at her watch. "Let's go," she said irritably. "I don't want to be late back."

Beatrice sat forward in her seat, gripped the steering wheel tightly, and peered over the top. Slowly the car chugged out of the yard and climbed the lane to the wood, backfiring loudly.

"Well, I'll be blowed. Maureen! Are you there, Maureen? Come and see what this boy has brought in."

It was hot in town but even hotter in the cluttered toyshop. Every available surface was covered with miniature cars, dolls, soft animals, balls. Against the walls were stacked buckets and spades, cricket and football sets, while on every wall shelves held stacks of jigsaws, construction kits and games. Under the counter, protected by glass, stood a doll's house and a spaceship complete with spacemen and buggies.

Andrew was used to going with Bella to the toy warehouse outside the town at home, where the toys were tiered on metal shelving, already packed in boxes, and you shopped with a supermarket trolley. This shop was like something out of an old children's book, an Aladdin's cave of surprises. He could have stayed there all day.

"Maureen!" the man yelled through the striped curtain at the back of the shop.

Bella hopped from one foot to another, now bending

down to peer into the doll's house, now stroking a furry donkey sitting on the counter.

Andrew's arms were aching under the weight of the farmyard. He'd felt self-conscious carrying the model across from the car park, down the high street to the toyshop.

"I'll take you to the toyshop, dear," Beatrice had said to Bella, after she had pointed it out as they drove into the town.

"No, I want to go with Andrew," Bella had declared. Even Bella seemed to have learnt now that where Andrew went Beatrice did not go.

An odd look had crept over Beatrice's face.

"I'm going to help Andrew sell it," said Bella importantly.

"Sell it?" said Beatrice, and for a moment Andrew thought she looked disappointed.

"So we can help Daddy. And I'm not going to ask for it for myself," added Bella piously. "We'll get lots of money instead and give it all to Daddy and then we might keep our house . . ."

Andrew watched the dust motes dancing in the sunlight that streamed through the shop's bay window. It was worse than waiting for his headmaster.

"Maureen, come and have a look at this!"

Sweat trickled down Andrew's neck inside his T-shirt. When he was making something, he knew it was his and it was the best he could do, but now he was laying it open for judgement. Well, if they didn't like it he could keep it for Bella's birthday.

A small woman with neat, grey curls pulled back the curtain. "What is it? Can't you manage alone?" she said irritably. Then she caught sight of the farm. She lifted a pair of glasses that hung on a cord around her neck and placed them on her nose. "Put it down, put it down."

Busily she cleared the toys off the counter, handing them to her husband beside her. Peering this way and that she examined the farm. She opened the gates and the barn doors, and then gave a cry of delight when she discovered the whole front wall of the farmhouse opened out like a doll's house.

Standing back, she took her glasses off and smiled first at her husband and then at Andrew.

"This is lovely, exquisite, my dear. And you made it?"

Andrew nodded with relief.

"I thought you'd like to see it, Maureen," said her husband, rubbing his hands as if the discovery was all his own work.

"Quite unique, isn't it?" said the woman smiling. "We get those farmhouses in a pack with a box for a farmhouse and a few animal pens, but I've never seen anything like this. It's like a doll's house and a farmyard all in one."

"It's modelled on a real farm," said Andrew quickly. "Only this roof should be thatch really . . ."

"Thatch," said the man. "Now that would be something, don't you think, Maureen?"

"It would be absolutely perfect," said the woman. "The finishing touch. And then we could put miniature furniture in the house, and animals in the farm. Something new for Christmas – we could display it in the front window."

"Where's that miniature tractor we had, I wonder?" said the man.

He pushed a step ladder against the wall and climbed up and pulled down a brown box. His wife was collecting farm animals off the shelves and arranging them in the barns and yard.

Bella frowned as the woman arranged tiny doll's furniture in the farmhouse as if it were theirs already.

"We want a lot of money," announced Bella.

Andrew kicked her from behind.

The woman looked up and peered over her glasses. "And what do you know about money, my dear?" she said, with a bright little laugh. "I think we would like a few curtains too, you know, a few little soft furnishings, perhaps a flowered chintz at the windows in the bedrooms, a few little finishing touches."

Just like Bella to go straight to the point. Now Andrew didn't know how to bring up the subject. "I'll have to take it back to think how to thatch it . . . and there are some other things I haven't finished."

"You do that, lad," said the man. "Get it to us when you can. If it sells – and I have a mind it will – we might take another."

The woman admired her handiwork and then started taking the animals and doll's furniture out. "A different one, I think," she murmured. "They must each be unique. But I do like the idea of thatch." She let her glasses fall down on to her pink blouse and stared briskly at Andrew. "Sale or return."

Thank goodness he'd helped Dad out in the holidays on his sales rounds. At least he didn't look as if he had no idea what he was up to.

"All right," Andrew said, delighted they were really going to take it, but trying to look as if this happened to him all the time. "I'll take it back if it doesn't sell. What will you sell it for?"

"We'll try for a hundred and twenty-five pounds, but you would get seventy-five."

Andrew could hardly believe his ears. He struggled to look calm but his ears were burning.

"I know it sounds a lot we're taking," went on the woman, "but it will take up a good bit of space in the window so we can't put other toys in, and our overheads with a high-street site are quite terrible these days."

She had misunderstood Andrew's hesitation. He picked up the farmyard and it suddenly felt lighter than he remembered – he could have been walking on air.

"Andrew will have seventy-five pounds if they sell the farmyard and they said they will. Is seventy-five pounds a lot of money? I asked for a lot of money. And it's all for Daddy. But Andrew's got to make some curtains for the windows." Bella chatted on as they drove out of the town.

Joanna watched the road impatiently as if she couldn't wait to get home. Beatrice listened and nodded.

It would all be worth it, this miserable summer, thought

Andrew, if he sold the farmyard. He hadn't felt so happy and excited for ages. He couldn't wait to find Simeon and tell him.

The car chugged into the yard. They were not alone. In front of the barns was parked a freshly polished car, with POLICE along its side.

"That'll be about the fire," said Beatrice with satisfaction. "Put the model in the barn, Andrew, and come straight to the house."

A policeman had called the day before. He had disappeared into the hayfield and left within half an hour. Through the door of the barn, Andrew had seen the police car arrive.

The voices that emerged from the sitting room now were different. He knocked on the door.

"It's the boy," said Beatrice. "Come along now."

Andrew pushed open the door. Sunk in the sagging velvet sofa was a young policeman with long legs. His bony knees were almost level with his face and he was trying to balance a notebook on top of them. Beside him, sitting upright on the edge of the sofa, was a policewoman, small and neat, with fair hair tied back from her face.

"Sit down . . . er . . ."

"Andrew Dunlop."

The policeman sat staring at his notebook with pencil ready to strike.

". . . the report is clear on that point," continued the policewoman to Beatrice. "The fire was started deliberately, as you suspected."

Beatrice nodded towards Andrew and sniffed. He might have been something objectionable the cat had brought in.

"You say that young Andrew here borrowed matches without asking, 'forgot' them, and then you found them returned after the fire."

"Yes," said Beatrice.

Andrew leant forward eagerly from his bristly chair by the wall. "I did borrow the matches to use for my model but I had nothing to do with the fire." He frowned. "You can't believe that, Beatrice."

He willed Beatrice to look at him from her seat in the cavernous old chair beside the piano. Slowly, and as if reluctantly, she turned towards him. Her small grey eyes, sunk in the wrinkled folds of her face, met his eyes momentarily and then looked away. It was as if she was trying hard to be angry, and yet her face showed more confusion than anger.

"Perhaps you can help us, Andrew," said the policewoman briskly. "Let's start at the beginning. Did you take the box of matches from the kitchen?"

"Yes. I wanted a few to spread the glue on to my model with – the model I've been making in the barn."

The policeman's pencil scratched neatly across the notebook.

"Why didn't you return the matches?"

"I forgot. I don't know. If they *had* been there, I'm sure I would have seen them and remembered . . ."

The policewoman waited, smiling slightly.

"Yet they were there after the fire. How was that?"

"I put them back."

"There you are," pronounced Beatrice triumphantly. "I said —"

The policewoman put up her hand. "Please ... Let Andrew speak. Tell me, Andrew, how could you have put them back if you had lost them?"

"I had lost them, only my friend found them."

"Simeon?" said Beatrice.

"Did your friend say where he found the matches?" The policewoman was leaning forward, her face intent.

"On the edge of a field. He found them as he was coming over here. Most of them had dropped out though."

The policewoman smiled at the policeman who nodded back and snapped the notebook shut.

"That will be all for now, Andrew. Miss Lofthouse, the fire investigator found matches, both new and used, lying beneath the hay thrown off the haystack."

"Simeon..." murmured Beatrice. "I should have guessed. Well," she continued addressing the room, "if it's not one boy, it's another. And if I hadn't been such a fool as to take in Andrew here, Simeon would have stayed away."

"We mustn't make accusations, Miss Lofthouse," said the policewoman, "until we have examined all the evidence, but we shall obviously need to interview Simeon and check out his story with Andrew's version. However, I don't think it's going to be too difficult to sort this one out."

The policeman pulled himself up out of the sofa, picked up his navy cap with its shiny police badge and set it on his head, then caught the policewoman's eye and snatched it off again.

"Boys will be boys," he said with a weak smile as he passed a grim-faced Beatrice on his way out.

Andrew stood with Beatrice at the door and watched the police car leave. His T-shirt felt cold and clammy for the second time that day. He must have been pouring sweat.

"Well, I'm thankful it wasn't you," said Beatrice. "I wouldn't like to have added to your mother's troubles. And . . . I would have been disappointed. As for that boy Simeon, I shall tell Peter I won't have him on my premises again, always slipping in and out of places he has no business to be. They're a rough lot, those two. I should have kept a closer eye on them."

"Gramps? Simeon? But Simeon's blind."

Beatrice snorted. "That boy's got eyes in his fingers. Nothing slips past him. I'll be bound he took the missing hens."

"But you said a fox . . ."

"Yes, a fox got in all right, but a fox can't unlatch a gate. Someone opened the gate first. Whoever did it presumably got a few for their own oven before the fox took his pickings."

Slowly it dawned on Andrew that Beatrice was talking as if he had not let the hens out or set the haystack alight. She was talking as if she believed him.

· Chapter Eight ·

Beatrice had had no time to cook lunch, but the table was spread with her purchases of the morning. The bread was fresh and crusty, still smelling of the bakery, and there was a new pat of butter. A big wedge of yellow farmhouse cheese lay beside slices of moist pink ham. And she added a pot of the sweet pickle that Andrew loved. She had sent Bella to pick raspberries when the police were there. The basin of fruit lay beside a bowl of cream thick enough to stand a spoon in.

Andrew wanted to eat but he couldn't. His appetite had fled and he felt low and depressed. He should have been feeling on top of the world now that Beatrice at last believed him, but he didn't.

Joanna crumbled her cheese and left the fresh bread half eaten.

"Appetite of a bird today, Joanna," said Beatrice. "Try these raspberries, my dear. Bella has picked them specially."

Bird, my foot, thought Andrew. Beatrice seemed to think Joanna mucking around with her food was a sign of ladylike delicacy or something. He remembered Joanna tucking in to her birthday supper – no bird there. She'd become such a poseur. But she was looking thin, now he thought about it. He hadn't noticed before.

Beatrice was smiling at both Joanna and Andrew. She was telling Joanna about Simeon and how she would never trust "that lot" again, and how horrified she was that she had allowed Andrew and Simeon "to get so thick".

Joanna looked up to meet Andrew's stare, and – he couldn't believe it – she smiled back at him. Everyone seemed to like him now. He wasn't used to it. He'd been on his own so long it felt strangely cloying, as if he was struggling to lift his feet in a mire of honey.

"It was my fault," Beatrice droned on.

She'd left Andrew to his own devices too much. If you wanted to stop a boy turning out badly you had to check on his friends and his activities, and not leave him alone unsupervised. But now Andrew would be needed for the harvest as she certainly wasn't going to let that boy Simeon near the place again. As for Peter ... She had no choice but to keep him this year, but she'd make other arrangements for the logs in future. Once the harvest was in they'd all have a nice day out at the sea together.

Andrew wanted to shout, "Stop it!" He couldn't think straight with Beatrice going on and on, and Joanna smiling at him so strangely.

Gramps had said they'd brought the logs because Simeon had known Andrew had arrived at the farm. How had he known? He must have been around spying, but he was blind, he couldn't see. Had he hidden behind a tree in the orchard and heard Andrew come out with Bella? He'd have heard Bella screaming when the cock bit her, and he would also have heard Bella say that Beatrice hated Andrew. Could he have guessed Andrew would be blamed when the hens got out?

Perhaps, too, Simeon had been hoping Andrew would be out when he brought the matches back. He was going to slip them on to the workbench and Andrew would never have understood why he hadn't seen them when he searched for them.

"Never again," Beatrice was saying. "Never again will I have that boy here."

She turned and smiled nervously at Andrew. The smile still lingered on Joanna's face too.

Andrew should have felt accepted, that he belonged at last, but he felt sick. He had lost Simeon.

Then he realised what it was. Joanna's smile had no warmth in it. It was the smile that drew you in and forced you to share in some exclusive friendship. There were boys like that at school, who only smiled with you at someone else's expense, with a cold, sly smile that excluded and ostracised those beyond its range.

Of course Simeon didn't do it! Why did he even try to believe it? Simeon said he had stood on the matchbox. He would never have stood on the box if he had carefully taken it and intended to slip it back. And why on earth would Simeon want to steal a few hens? He would have found it impossible to grab a chicken unless he could see it. They ran as soon as they saw you coming.

Andrew's thoughts raced ahead, like feet shaking off the sweet and sticky mire, at last able to move again.

Simeon wasn't the sort of boy to get a thrill from setting a haystack alight or stealing a few hens, when he had all the fields and woods to explore. He hung around the farm because he wanted to be friends. And that was what Andrew wanted above all else – Simeon to talk to, to muck about with, to share things with, because he had no one else now.

Had the police been to Simeon? Simeon would think Andrew had accused him, tried to blame him.

Andrew shook himself. What had he done? He cut himself two doorsteps of bread and crammed a thick slice of ham between them. He was starving.

When lunch was over and washed up, Andrew slipped out to the barn as he usually did, to work on the model. He couldn't wait to get to Simeon and explain before he lost his one decent friend, but somehow he had to get away unobserved. Ignoring the little farmyard, he hung back in the shadow of the barn door, where he couldn't be seen, and watched the kitchen door. He could hear Beatrice and Bella chatting.

"We'll not go out in this heat," said Beatrice. "I shall rest on my bed, and so should you, Bella."

"But I'm not tired, Beatrice."

"You can play quietly in your room then. It's much too hot for walking. We'll take a picnic tea to the heath later."

"Can Andrew come with us?"

"He'll be busy at his model no doubt, but you can ask him. That book we looked at . . . "

The voices faded and Andrew could hear footsteps on the stairs.

He hurried out, across the yard and into the orchard. The air was cooler beneath the old trees. The chickens were pecking in the shade and Sam lay slumped beneath an apple tree, one eye open. As soon as he saw Andrew's hurrying feet he heaved himself up with interest and wagged his tail. Andrew was glad to have Sam's company.

He hadn't been to Simeon's house before, but he knew that he and Gramps lived further round the heath.

He edged round the wheatfield, hardly registering the scratch of the bramble trails in his path. The corn was golden now and bending at the top of the stems. He climbed the gate while Sam squeezed through a gap in the hedge, and surveyed the hayfield. He hadn't been there since the fire. The haystack was charred and looked as if vandals had attacked it. One end was completely burnt away and blackened hay lay scattered over the grass, but most of it had been saved, Andrew was relieved to see.

The heath spread out beneath the woods, hugging the base of the hill. Andrew and Sam set off at a quick pace round the brow of the hill. The heat was searing: there was no shade. The dog panted, pink tongue lolling.

"Go back, Sam," said Andrew. "You don't have to come." He patted Sam's sleek black head. It was nice to be loved by someone so uncomplicated and simple. Sam gave Andrew a mournful look and plodded on beside him.

The bees rose up around them and butterflies darted ahead as they disturbed the grass in their hurry. It was difficult to make out the far side of the heath because of the hazy mirage thrown up by the heat, but Andrew thought he could see something square shimmering in the distance.

Sam stopped, lifted his head in the air, and barked tentatively. From over the brow of the heath came an answering bark. Wagging his tail furiously, Sam leapt ahead, the heat forgotten.

As Andrew jogged closer, a tiny thatched cottage came into view. There was a central door gleaming with new brown paint, a tiny matching window on each side of the door, and one window on the floor above. The thatch was dark with age, but lighter patches here and there showed where it had been recently repaired.

The cottage stretched across one side of a small plot. In front of the house the grass was cut short and edged with a border of bright flowers. The old lorry was parked between neat stacks of logs and an ancient shed, also patched with newer timbers of a lighter colour.

It was so different from the farm, where everything was run down and decrepit. Here somebody cared, and looked after the place.

A small mongrel came bounding up to Sam, barking playfully and with tail wagging. So much for loving Andrew – Sam had come to see his friend.

Andrew's sense of urgency drained away as he stared at the cottage. Everything had seemed so clear and easy when he set out, but now he couldn't think what he was going to say.

Under a spreading ash tree at the side of the grass sat a little group. They were seated round an old pine kitchen table set with mugs and a pot of tea. The dappled shade sent quivering shadows over the backs of Simeon and a woman with a long black plait, who glanced over her shoulder at Andrew and then looked away. Gramps, alone in the full sun, watched Andrew silently, with no word of welcome.

"I'm sorry to barge in," he said awkwardly.

No one answered or offered him a seat.

"I just came to say . . . I know Simeon didn't do it."

Still no one spoke and Simeon's back remained resolutely turned.

Gramps moved first, and tugged at his beard.

"Is that what you told the police?" His voice was gruff and harsh.

"I didn't say Simeon did it, but I didn't deny it either."

"Fair-weather friend, are you then?" said Gramps.

"No," said Andrew, his voice rising, "I'm not. I don't know why I didn't say anything."

"As simple as that, was it?" said Gramps. "Get rid of the police by sending them round here, eh? A nice scene for Simeon's mother to find when she comes to see her son. The police questionin' him an' all."

"I'm sorry, truly I am," said Andrew quietly. "What did the police say?"

"Simeon told them frontwards, backwards an' upside-down what he did on the day of the fire. There was nothin' to catch him out with."

"So it's all right?" said Andrew hesitantly. "You see, when I thought about it with the police there and Beatrice and then Joanna, I got so muddled. I . . . I thought Simeon might have done it."

Simeon turned towards the dark-haired woman with the plait over her shoulder. His back was all Andrew could see.

"I couldn't help it. It was as if something was sticking me down, making me believe it, so that it wasn't my fault, and . . . " Andrew's voice trailed to a whisper . . . "so that Beatrice and Joanna would like me."

Nobody answered.

"But I got clear in time. I knew I had been nuts to even think it. I came to say sorry, Simeon."

Gramps and the woman looked at Simeon.

"It's all right," said Simeon. "It's that girl, I expect. She wanted you to get rid of me."

"Joanna?"

Why did everything come back to Joanna? She never said anything, but she had smiled, and briefly Andrew had felt warm and welcomed, joined in some conspiracy of acceptance.

"Tell me, Simeon." The woman with the dark plait bent her face close to Simeon.

She had a handsome profile with a fine, pointed chin, down which dangled a long gold earring that shone against her sun-browned skin.

"It's not really my story," said Simeon. "Andrew can tell." She turned to stare at Andrew with the same dark, conker-brown eyes as Simeon, but they were eyes that looked at Andrew and saw.

Gramps pulled up an old kitchen chair for Andrew and fetched another mug from the cottage. Andrew looked across at Simeon as he sat with his arm wound through his mother's, fingering her rows of bracelets. Suddenly he felt very homesick and he was glad to tell.

Simeon's mother sat still, attentive. It all sounded so silly but she didn't laugh. Here and there she interrupted Andrew to ask a question. When he sat back, exhausted from telling, she waited, deep in thought, before turning to Gramps.

"Dad, when do you start the harvest?"

"I reckon the day after tomorrow is likeliest, but Miss Beatrice has the last word on that."

Simeon's mother leant forward across the table and clasped Andrew's hand. The rings on her fingers were cool against his sweaty palm. "You have very little time," she said, her dark eyebrows drawn together in a frown.

Gramps looked at his daughter. "You reckon so?" he said gravely. "I thought on it too. Sent Simeon up with the boy to get his sister out the other day – always up in the woods, tryin' to get in the maze she is. We sees her pass, don't we, Simeon?"

Simeon nodded.

"Very little time for what?" asked Andrew, staring from one serious face to another.

"It's a strange tale," said Simeon's mother, tossing her shining plait back over her shoulder. "I've not seen it happen in my lifetime and nor had my mother."

"Nor she had," nodded Gramps, "but I heard her tell it often."

"Tell what?" Andrew implored.

"Listen," Simeon's mother said as she released Andrew's palm. Her brown eyes stared into Andrew's. "The maze is old, too old for any man to record, from before the time of the Christians. Then, so my mother said, it was a place holy to the Celtic people and their pagan Druids. Only the Druid priests entered the grove and only they knew the way through the maze to their altar."

"Were they bad?" asked Andrew anxiously.

"Not bad ... They were clever men and women, who understood the movements of the stars and mathematics. They were powerful and held sway over the chieftains and counselled their people with wise advice, but they believed in gods that got angry and needed sacrifices to appease them."

"But Joanna ...?"

Simeon's mother lifted her hand. "Wait. Listen to what I know. My mother told me what she had been told when she was a girl, that there have been times of cold and wet summers when the harvest is rotting and near to being lost, when Tailltu, the goddess of the harvest, demands a gift to do her part and restore the harvest. It must be a boy or girl, unspoilt by the world, good and kind, and if by chance they stray into the grove at the time when the harvest is close to ruin, she will claim the boy or girl as her own. It is the fair price for turning the wheat gold."

"But she didn't take Joanna," said Andrew. "She's still with us, only she's turned nasty."

"Exactly," said Simeon's mother. "Tailltu draws the goodness from her, little by little, and feeds it to the harvest. In the space that is left there is only room for evil to flourish."

Andrew didn't want to believe what he was hearing, but he knew Simeon's mother was saying truthfully what she had heard. It fitted. It seemed right.

"But Gramps said the harvest is the day after tomorrow. What will happen to Joanna?"

"When the goodness is close to gone, Tailltu will call your sister and take her. Then the harvest will be ready."

"Take her – What do you mean?"

"I don't know, but I know they don't come back."

"Who doesn't come back?"

"The gift, the sacrifice."

Andrew sat slumped in his chair, the tea growing cold, untouched in front of him. He hadn't a clue what to do. His mother would never believe him even if he told her. She'd think he'd gone mad or something. At the back of his mind Andrew could hear his father's voice repeating again and again, like a disc that had got stuck: "I'm relying on you." He clutched his head in his hands.

"Andrew." Simeon got up and felt his way round the table to Andrew. "We mustn't let her get to the maze. It's obvious that's why she keeps on going up there. This Tailltu thing must be calling her."

Yes . . . Joanna couldn't help herself. They had to help her. Had she . . . had she . . .?

"Simeon, do you think Joanna let the chickens out to get me into trouble?"

"Did she want everyone to believe I started the fire when she did it herself?" said Simeon sadly.

"Better not to ask now," said Gramps, clattering the mugs together. "If there's more trouble we'll have to say, but no one should accuse without proof. And as for whether there is anythin' in this Romany tale, well, it beats me. But keep an eye on that sister of yours, young Andrew. No more strayin' all over the place on her own, not till the harvest's done."

"Can Simeon come and . . .?"

"No!"

The fierceness of Gramps' reply stunned Andrew.

"No. Just afore you came we had that sister of yours here . . ."

"Joanna?"

"The big 'un."

"Simeon, is this true?"

Simeon nodded.

"Miss Beatrice sent her," said Gramps. "All ladylike and up in the clouds she was, too good for the likes of us. And: 'Beatrice says Simeon is not to set foot on the farm ever again,' she says."

"Mum tried to talk to her," said Simeon. "She was only trying to be friendly, but . . . but . . . Joanna just went on and on: 'Beatrice says Simeon is not to set foot on the farm ever again.' "

"Something was wrong," murmured Simeon's mother. "I could see that."

Now Andrew understood the hostility of the little group under the tree. Cold-shouldered by Joanna, shopped to the police by himself . . .

Andrew leapt guiltily to his feet. Gramps wouldn't let Simeon come. He was on his own now. He turned to go, struggling to hold back the tears he didn't want. He must get back – to Joanna.

"Hold on, lad," said Gramps. His voice was gruff but kind. "I'll just put this tea away and I'll come with you."

Andrew stared at him in surprise.

"We'll go up to the wheatfield below the heath. That way we can catch that sister of yours if she passes."

"What will Beatrice say if she sees — "

"Simeon says you are wantin' to thatch that model of yours. We'll collect a bit of wheat – there's always some broken off at the edges and Miss Beatrice can't count every blade. I'll show you how it's done." Gramps pointed up at the neatly patched thatch on the cottage roof. "And, Simeon, take your mother up to the maze for a nice evening walk, and if you meet the girl— "

"We'll frighten her off," said Simeon with feeling.

Simeon's mother laid a restraining arm round his shoulders.

"Try and keep her away," pleaded Andrew. "I'll watch her at the farm but if she gets through . . . "

"She won't," said Simeon. "We won't let her."

"Simeon, I won't be able to come and see you till after the harvest."

Without the prospect of seeing Simeon Andrew felt quite alone, even though Gramps walked beside him and the two dogs leaped and chased around them.

· Chapter Nine ·

Andrew dropped the bundles of fallen wheat he and Gramps had collected on the table in the barn. They had watched the path round the wheatfield all the time, but Joanna had not come past. Hesitantly, he went towards the voices that drifted through the kitchen door.

Beatrice and Bella were packing up a picnic for their walk. They looked relaxed and fresh after their rest.

"Where's Joanna?"

Beatrice shrugged her shoulders. "Walking out alone, no doubt. She likes to go her own way. Have you seen her, Bella?"

Bella shook her head.

Beatrice picked up a pot of jam and spooned strawberries on to a slice of bread. "I've a mind that girl is too much alone. You should go with her, Andrew, instead of hanging round with that boy Simeon."

"She doesn't want me to," said Andrew. "She avoids me. Beatrice, could I have some cotton thread and some pins? I won't forget them this time. I'll bring them straight back when I've finished."

Beatrice straightened up and hobbled over to her mending basket on the dresser. She didn't even ask why he wanted them.

"It's for the thatch."

"Let me see it when you've finished," said Beatrice. "Thatch isn't easy."

"Gramps has told me how to do it."

Beatrice turned and stared at him. Why had he mentioned Gramps?

"I said you were to have no more to do with Peter and Simeon."

"You're wrong, Beatrice," blurted out Andrew. "I know Simeon hasn't done half the things you think."

"Who did then?"

Andrew couldn't bring himself to say Joanna. After all, he didn't know for sure.

"Beatrice, did you know the maze in the woods was made by Druids?"

"So some locals say."

"And that if it's an awful summer and the harvest is rotten, the harvest goddess takes someone and sort of squeezes all the goodness out of her and puts it back in the harvest, and she gets more and more evil, until the harvest is ready and then . . ." Andrew's voice trailed off. He was afraid that if he voiced what might happen it really would happen.

"What do you mean 'she'? I hope you've not got anyone in mind. It's all old folk nonsense."

"But you know it rained all summer. Do you remember when it stopped raining and the good weather started?"

"The day we came!" shouted Bella. "I wanted a wee and Joanna and I went up into the wood and it rained and rained, but when we came out the sun was shining and Mum had to go."

Beatrice was listening, curious and intent. Then: "I've got this too," she said suddenly, as if to shake off unwelcome thoughts. She handed Andrew an old carrier bag. He peered in. It was full of scraps of material.

"What is it?"

"Bella said you had to make curtains for the farm."

It was no use going up to the maze unless he knew for sure Joanna had gone there. Besides, Simeon and his mother would be there watching. He was best staying close to the farm. He'd wait for Joanna to come back and then not let her out of his sight again.

Andrew dragged his work table closer to the door. In the barn he couldn't be seen, but he could watch the yard outside. The model was looking good. He cut the wheat stalks into short bundles and tied each bundle with cotton. Starting with the bottom edge, he pinned each bundle to the roof, bending the pin over at either side to hold the bunch of stalks in place. When the first row was complete he started on the second. The new row hid the cotton and pins. It looked terrific, like real thatch.

By the time Beatrice called him in Andrew could hardly see what he was doing, but he had almost completed the whole of one side of the roof. He was so engrossed that he jumped at Beatrice's voice behind him.

"You shouldn't work in such bad light. My goodness, that does look good."

"Do you think so?" said Andrew, delighted.

"Bella is asleep already, and Joanna is up in her room," said Beatrice quickly and limped to the door.

So Joanna hadn't gone out at all. He hadn't thought of that. But, what was worse, he had been so absorbed with the thatching that he had almost forgotten her.

He ran through the kitchen and up the stairs. Beatrice was already in her room, moving around, but there was no sound from Joanna's room. Andrew tapped and pushed the door open. Joanna was sitting on the window seat, staring out into the deepening night. She was still in her clothes.

"Beatrice said you'd gone up already," said Andrew nervously.

"What business is it of yours?" said Joanna. "Get out. I don't come into your room."

The locket on her chest glinted in the gloom and her eyes seemed to light up with an echoing fire.

Andrew closed the door quietly. He knew better now than to argue. Nothing surprised him any more.

He went up to his room and sat fully clothed on his bed. Whatever happened he mustn't sleep tonight, or tomorrow night either. Simeon and Gramps might help listen and watch in the day but the night was his responsibility and his alone.

Andrew jerked awake, cramped up against the brass bedstead, and rubbed his shoulder. He must have dozed off. All trace of twilight was gone and his room was in darkness, but through the window the silver light of the moon had picked out his gleaming bedstead and woken him.

Below him a floorboard creaked. A door opened cautiously, and a light step crossed the landing to the stairs. He'd heard it before, he was sure. Of course – it all flooded back to him – it was the first night after he had shut up the chickens!

Wide awake now, Andrew lowered his feet to the floor and listened. Nothing stirred. Whoever it was had gone out. He tiptoed down the attic stairs and into Joanna's room. The door was open.

"Joanna?" Andrew whispered.

The bed had not been slept in and the window seat was empty.

Andrew rushed to the window and peered out. Beneath him a figure flitted past the farm and through the orchard, towards the gate leading to the wheatfield. As quickly and quietly as he could, Andrew ran down the stairs and out through the kitchen.

It was a clear and hot night, with a full yellow moon still low in the sky. Day-time colours had faded but the moon lit up the farm in greys and silvers, transforming the barns and yard into a strange and menacing world. Dark trees in the orchard stood sentinel in a prickly sea of silver grass. As Andrew climbed the gate into the wheatfield he could hear little scuffles and rustlings in the hedgerow.

Joanna must be going to the maze. He had to stop her. What if it was tonight that Tailltu claimed her due? He wasn't sure he could manage alone, without Gramps or Simeon to help him.

The grass was wet with dew. Soon the bottoms of

Andrew's jeans were drenched. He was halfway up the heath path when he heard a snort and breathing behind him. He spun round.

"Sam! Did I wake you up?"

Andrew laid his hand on the dog's heaving back. He was glad Sam had heard him and that he was no longer alone.

When they got to the trees, the path disappeared into the beeches. He must find the route Simeon had led him. The path seemed to peter out in a soft bed of beech mast. Andrew continued in the direction he thought he remembered, until he and Sam reached the black wall of yews. How had he and Simeon got past them?

Andrew pushed through as best he could, ducking low branches, beating at the mosquitoes whining in his ears. It was no good. He was only zig-zagging backwards and forwards. His heart thumped like a stopwatch, marking the seconds of the fleeting minutes since Joanna had gone.

"It's no good, Sam. We'll have to go back and find the path again."

Sam patiently followed Andrew as he headed downhill through the beech trees. The path had stopped there, Andrew was sure.

"Here goes, Sam. Second time lucky!"

But the dog was gone.

Andrew stared round about him and up at the dark roof of leaves above him.

"Sam? Come here!"

No answering bark or snuffle came back. Andrew shivered and knew he was afraid.

He stumbled over roots, his walk turning into a headlong run downhill. Out of the beeches, the yellow harvest moon lit up the heath beneath him. There was Sam ahead of him, running and leaping, his growls echoing faintly in the still night air, but holding himself back, never quite catching the running figure ahead of him.

Joanna! She'd been to the maze and back already. Andrew had missed her.

The thumping of his heart grew less as Andrew jogged steadily down the heath, through the hay- and wheatfields and into the orchard. Joanna must be tired out: with luck she'd be heading for bed.

He turned the corner into the yard and went across to the kitchen door. As he pushed the door open he heard a growl from across the yard.

"Sam!" called Andrew. "Do you want to come in, boy?"

Sam ignored the invitation and growled again.

"Where are you, Sam? I can't see you."

The growl came from the barn.

"What's up? Have you got a rat?"

Andrew strode over to the barn and peered in.

For a moment he could see nothing in the thick blackness, but he could hear Sam panting close beside him. Then, he saw, standing in a beam of moonlight shining through the hole in the roof, Joanna. In her hand she held up Andrew's hammer.

The hand came down – smash! – to the sound of splintering wood.

"Joanna!" Andrew screamed. He tripped over something

as he lunged towards her. Half falling, he butted against her, grabbing her arm as it lifted again. "Let go!" he shouted.

He wrenched the hammer from her hand threw it as far away as he could. "Why did you do it?" he screamed. "I don't care if you hate me, but it was for Dad, to help Dad!"

A beam of yellow light flooded through the barn from the door.

"What *is* going on?" came Beatrice's angry voice. She focused her torch in a blinding dazzle on Andrew and Joanna. "You two should have been in bed long ago."

Joanna slipped past and through the door without a word.

Andrew was shaking. "She did it deliberately. I saw her," His chest heaved with a sob as he spoke. "I'm not going to look. I don't want to see. She's evil, evil."

Beatrice walked up to inspect his model. Then she raised her torch and shone it on Andrew.

"Andrew. Perhaps . . ."

"No!" Andrew cried, as he lifted his hands to protect his face from the dazzle. "No! Leave me alone!"

And he ran from the barn.

· Chapter Ten ·

Andrew hid his face in the pillow. He could hear voices in the yard and the raucous noise of an old engine being started. It was getting more and more difficult to get up and face a new day and today was the worst. He didn't want to see, or speak, or have anything to do with Joanna. He wanted to be rid of her and leave her on her own until Mum came. As for the model, he was not going into the barn again this holiday. The wreck could fall to pieces with everything else old and run down and rotten on the farm.

There was a knock on his door and he could hear Bella giggling outside.

"Who is it?"

The door swung open, and an antique wooden tray with legs appeared round the door, with Beatrice breathing heavily behind it.

Bella was bursting with excitement. "We've had breakfast ages ago," she said as she scrambled on to Andrew's bed.

"You get off that bed, my girl, else we'll have nowhere to put this tray."

Before Andrew's astonished eyes Beatrice set the legs upright on the blankets on either side of his knees.

"It's a busy day today. I thought you'd better not start without your breakfast."

Andrew stared at the glistening yellow eye of the fried egg, and breathed in the tantalising smell of crisp bacon and grilled sausage.

"Can I share your toast?" asked Bella. "I'm hungry again."

"You certainly won't, young lady. We've got work to do outside."

Beatrice gave her hand to Bella and pulled her away from the bed.

"Thanks!" Andrew whispered in amazement. "Beatrice, have . . . have you seen Joanna?"

Beatrice appeared not to hear his question as she closed the door behind her.

It took some getting used to, people being kind to him.

He was mopping up the last of the egg with a corner of toast when he heard steps again on the stairs up to the attic. They were slow, hesitant steps, not as heavy and lopsided as Beatrice's. Andrew waited for the door to open.

"Simeon! How did you get in?"

"She told me to come up and see you, if I could find the way to the attic."

"Beatrice?"

"Yes. When Gramps came over to get the combine ready she sent him straight back to fetch me."

"I can't believe it – breakfast, then you. Come and sit on the bed – you're not going to bump into anything. This room's as bare as a prison cell."

Simeon moved cautiously towards the bed, with his right hand held out in front of him.

"What are you eating?"

"Breakfast. You can have a piece of toast with the corner missing."

Simeon's hand felt the contents of the tray. "Who brought this lot up?"

"Beatrice! Simeon, I've got some bad news, really bad news."

"I know – Miss Beatrice took me in and showed me. She's given me the morning off so that I can help you check on the damage."

Andrew buttered the toast and smeared it with strawberry jam. "I don't think I want to see it."

"It's not that bad. The thatch you made is all messed up and there's a hole in the roof and a floor is splintered, but we should be able to repair it."

Andrew sighed with relief.

"I wasn't sure how long Joanna had been there. You know she smashed it with the hammer?"

"Miss Beatrice told me."

"She can only have hit it once before I stopped her."

The sun had moved round to shine on Andrew's bed. So the model was mendable. Bella's shouts and laughter mingled with Gramps' gruff voice and Beatrice's calmer tones in the yard below.

"Come on," said Andrew, "I want to get up. And . . . and I've got to check on Joanna."

The massive combine harvester in the yard was nothing like the one in Andrew's school geography book. It was a dirty yellow and rusting. There was no cabin with air-conditioning and radio, but only a seat on the top open to the sky and sun.

"Looks all right to me, Beatrice," Gramps shouted from the seat as the deafening roar of the engine died down. "Bit of oil and she'll bite like a lion."

"So you think she'll get us through the harvest this year?" said Beatrice anxiously. "She's looking her age, isn't she?"

"So are we all," said Gramps, pushing a battered straw hat back on his head. "But she'll go on for ever, just like us."

Beatrice laughed.

"What is it, Andrew?" she said, noticing Andrew by her side.

"The harvest – is it tomorrow?"

"We start as soon as the dew is dried. Ten o'clock I should think, wouldn't you, Peter?"

Gramps nodded and grinned.

"Where's Joanna?"

"Leave her, Andrew. She's not well. Didn't eat a scrap of breakfast. She's resting on her bed."

"You're sure?"

"You'll see her yourself if she comes out."

He should go and see her, he knew it. He wanted to forget her, to wash his hands of her, but he couldn't. He'd go later. If she was lying in her room, surely she'd be safe enough there.

Simeon was right about the model. The damage could

have been worse. Bella collected fresh wheat stems from the field, while Andrew prised off the roof, and measured new timber for the floor and roof. Simeon cut the stalks and tied them into uniform bundles. It was tremendous to have Simeon and Bella working around him, but Andrew was annoyed that he couldn't enjoy it more or keep his mind on the job. Half his mind was nagging at him, worrying him.

"Let's carry the model into the yard," he said. "We can sit in the sun and check that Joanna doesn't get out. We can't let her near the maze today."

By lunchtime the repairs were finished. Beatrice brought out lemonade and a pile of sandwiches.

"You can eat Joanna's as well. She doesn't want hers, and then I want you two boys to clean out the grain trailer."

Simeon and Andrew set to with a broom and hose to sweep out and wash down the trailer that would take the grain off the combine. Andrew swept and Simeon hosed.

"Simeon! Get that hose off me!" cried Andrew as a spray of icy water trickled down his back.

"I didn't see you," said Simeon innocently.

"Course you didn't, but you knew I was behind you." Andrew grabbed the hose and turned it on Simeon.

"Cut it out, you boys!" Gramps shouted. "There's work to be done round here."

They were drenched, but it was bliss in the heat.

"This is the hottest day yet," groaned Andrew.

But he couldn't forget Joanna, try as he might. "Joanna's not come out. Perhaps she got sunstroke or something yesterday. There are books about people getting sunstroke in the desert and behaving strangely."

"Since when has Dorset been a desert?"

"I'm only trying to think of other reasons," said Andrew angrily. "Listen, Simeon, how am I going to stop her getting out? I tried to keep awake last night but I dozed off. I can't stop myself."

"I'll stay. We can sleep in the barn together tonight, then we can take turns to listen."

"We might both fall asleep," said Andrew anxiously. "She's so sly now. She slips out so quietly we may never notice her. I'm worried out of my mind, Simeon – and I'm worried because sometimes I think I don't care any longer – but what if something dreadful happens to her and I could have stopped it?"

"You must care, Andrew," said Simeon, dropping the hose. "Your not caring is what Tailltu would want. You'd be playing into her hands. We've got to fight it."

"But how can we fight her? We can't be sure she won't find Joanna if she wants her that much."

"If she wants her that much we must find something else as good."

"What do you mean?"

"If we keep Joanna back, surely we ought to give another gift instead or else some awful revenge might happen."

"Simeon, you don't think – I didn't think of that – we should give something special of Joanna's?"

"It would have to be something that only Joanna has."

Andrew sat down on the end of the trailer and swung his legs over the edge. "She's always wearing this gold locket Mum and Dad gave her for her birthday, but we couldn't give that. It was Mum's and my gran's."

Simeon sank down beside Andrew and felt for the edge of the trailer. Carefully he swung his feet over. "What's it got in it?"

"In it?"

"Lockets have twists of hair in or things to remember people by, don't they?"

"It's got an old picture of Joanna as a little girl, sitting on Dad's knee."

"There you are! You'll have to cut your dad out, though."

They sat in silence listening to the voices in the kitchen.

"It's special, and Joanna loves it and wears it all the time," murmured Andrew.

"But it's got her in it. Perhaps Tailltu . . . "

"I'll have to get it off her, though," said Andrew glancing towards the house. "And we'll have to take it to the maze and leave it there."

"What will we put it in?" said Simeon. "We can't just leave it lying on the grass. It needs a box, something to do with Joanna."

Andrew stared over at the model. It was sitting on the old table in the doorway of the barn. The thatch was golden and bright in the sunlight. The man in the toyshop was right – it was the perfect finishing touch for the farmyard. Now it looked like the real thing only better, with a gate that worked, gleaming fences, carefully pointed red bricks, not a tile missing from the barns and new curtains blowing at the windows. For once Andrew was glad Simeon couldn't see what he was looking at.

"You're looking at the model, aren't you?"

"How did you know?"

"I felt it. I could hear you thinking hard."

"What do you think?"

"It's where Joanna lives now. You haven't got any other home but the farm. Perhaps that's why she tried to destroy the model. It's her home and she's got to leave it to go to Tailltu. It's the most special thing you have."

"Shut up, Simeon."

Simeon lowered himself over the side of the trailer, hanging down with his hands, and then jumped to the ground. "Please yourself. She's not my sister."

"Wait, Simeon!" Andrew shouted. He jumped off the trailer. "Go into the kitchen and keep Beatrice talking until I'm back."

Andrew didn't bother to knock. He turned the doorknob as slowly as he could and pushed the door open. The curtains were drawn across the window so that the room was shady and felt cold after the heat outside. Throughout the room there was a musty smell of old and decaying things.

A slow breathing came from the bed.

Joanna was curled up on the cover, fast asleep. Andrew could see now how thin and fragile she had become. Her face was paler than he remembered, despite all her walks outside. Her lips were slightly apart and a faint shade of blue. His anger and his desire to be rid of her evaporated and he was overwhelmed with a dreadful and crushing need to protect her.

One of Joanna's hands lay curled on the pillow beside her, while the other lay on her chest, clasping the gold locket at her neck. How could he get the locket without waking her? He looked around and saw the toothbrush in the mug on the dressing table. That would do it.

He worked the handle of the toothbrush into the palm of her hand, following the path of the locket chain. Joanna stirred. She turned over so that the hand holding the locket was now pressed against the pillow.

Again Andrew pushed with the toothbrush, gently levering her fingers apart. Quickly he lifted the chain and locket over her face. Joanna's fingers gripped tightly on the toothbrush as if it was the locket. Andrew didn't dare try to pull it out.

"Been to see Joanna?" Beatrice asked as she cut into the fresh chocolate cake on the table.

"She's asleep."

"Best leave her. That girl's not well today. Peter, have you eaten that slice already?"

"Another cup of tea would suit me fine, Beatrice, and if you're offerin' more of the cake, I won't be sayin' no."

"And for me, for me," pleaded Bella.

"Where's that 'please', my girl? We've got to feed up the harvesters first. They'll need all the energy they can get tomorrow. Andrew, take these out for you and Simeon. He's fiddling with the model."

"I'm a harvester, aren't I? I'm going to help . . . "

Bella's voice followed Andrew out of the door. After the cold shade of Joanna's room the kitchen had been alive with sunlight and cheerful faces. The agricultural engineer had been called to re-align the blades. The diesel for the old fuel tank had been delivered by a man with a florid face. Together with Gramps they had demolished Beatrice's cake. Andrew had never seen the farm so full of people, chattering and exuberant in anticipation of the next day. The harvest would be good after all, and they knew it. Andrew knew it too. Yet by the time Andrew reached the barn, he felt half-sick with dread of what was to come.

· CHAPTER ELEVEN ·

On Beatrice's instructions, Bella woke Joanna for supper.

"How are you feeling, my dear?" enquired Beatrice anxiously as Joanna stood at the bottom of the steps to the kitchen. "You've slept all day."

"I'm tired," said Joanna. "Someone's taken my locket."

Andrew stared at his plate.

"Nonsense, dear, nobody would take it without asking. It's probably fallen somewhere. We'll find it later," said Beatrice.

Joanna slumped into her chair at the table and stared at the plate of lamb chops and vegetables in front of her. "I'm not hungry."

"It's the heat that's getting to you; it's gone all sultry," said Beatrice, fanning herself with the oven cloth. "It's probably not the weather for a hot meal, but we've not eaten much today and it's the harvest tomorrow. We'll need all our strength. Try a little, dear."

Andrew watched Joanna wearily cut up her chop. She lifted her fork to her mouth, looked at it and put it down again.

"The peas are fresh from the garden," coaxed Beatrice, "sweet as sugar."

Joanna managed the odd mouthful, but it was like coaxing a sick animal to eat. Andrew had not seen her as bad as this. She'd grown worse over the last few days without him noticing; he'd been so intent on avoiding her.

"It's early to bed for us all tonight. We've a busy day tomorrow," said Beatrice.

Bella yawned.

"Up you go!"

Beatrice disappeared upstairs to supervise Bella into bed and Joanna followed soon afterwards.

Normally Andrew would have been fed up with being left with all the clearing up to do, but now he quickly scraped the one untouched lamb chop off Joanna's plate and on to a clean one and piled on the remaining potatoes and peas.

He listened at the foot of the stairs. Beatrice was chatting to Bella in the bathroom. Andrew went out through the open door, across the yard and into the barn.

"It's got a bit cold, but it looks all right," he said as he laid the plate on the workbench and guided Simeon's hand to the plate.

"It smells great," said Simeon. "Lamb . . . Is it a chop?"

"Yes."

"You can take the knife back. I'll never manage to cut the meat off the bone. I'll gnaw it."

Sam was lying at Simeon's feet. He lifted his nose and sniffed, and then put out his tongue and slobbered noisily.

"OK, Sam," said Simeon. "You can have the bone."

"They're all going to bed," said Andrew. "Joanna's gone too. We'll have to get up to the maze before she decides to go."

"But we don't know if she'll go or even when she'll go," said Simeon. "She could get out before we're ready."

"I've thought of that," said Andrew. "She doesn't usually go out until after dark. As soon as Beatrice has turned out her light we'll barricade Joanna in."

They didn't have long to wait. Beatrice came to her window, pushed it open and leant out. The sun's last rays caught her face, giving her a golden glow, and she was smiling. She looked happier than Andrew had ever seen her. The curtains were pulled across and the light went out.

"It's getting darker," whispered Andrew as he rescued the plate Sam had licked clean from the barn floor.

"About time too," said Simeon. "I'm bored stiff waiting here."

They crossed the yard, went through the tidied kitchen and tiptoed up the stairs until they stood on the landing. Andrew put a finger against Simeon's lips and then guided his hand to the dark wooden linen cupboard that stood to one side of Joanna's door. He bent his face to Simeon's ear.

"It's big. A sort of chest on top of a chest, full of old blankets. It's a dead weight. We'll have to slide it. I'll pull it and you push."

They held on to the sides, each end.

"Now," whispered Andrew.

With a dreadful creaking the cupboard moved halfway across the door. Andrew stopped, petrified, but there was no response from Joanna's room or from Beatrice. For one awful moment he wondered if Joanna had left already. He couldn't look now. They had to finish the job.

"Again," he whispered.

He pulled until his arms ached and the cupboard edged across and covered the doorframe.

Simeon stretched up his hands and stood on tiptoe. Carefully he felt either side of the doorframe. He nudged Andrew and gave a thumbs up.

Andrew pulled Simeon's arm down. They had to get away and on with the next stage of the plan.

Back in the barn, Simeon ran his hands over the model farmyard. "It's all ready. You've got the locket?"

Andrew pulled the locket from his pocket. It dangled at the end of its chain, glinting in the fading light. He prised open the back with his thumbnail and could just make out the round, laughing face of a little girl. Her cheeks were plump and creased at the edges by the smiling mouth. He looked in disbelief. That was the Joanna he remembered, although from the year before he was born, better than the aloof sister he had now.

She was sitting on Dad's knee, dwarfed by his massive chest. Dad was looking down at her, smiling proudly.

Andrew took the scissors off the table, dug out the photo and cut round Dad's knees, chest and head until only the tiny toddler remained. Joanna he slipped back into the locket which he snapped shut. Dad lay, cut out in the palm of Andrew's hand.

You won't let me down, son. The words echoed through Andrew's head.

"No," Andrew said. "I won't."

"Won't what?" said Simeon. "I thought we'd agreed we'd put the locket in the model."

"I'll keep it in my pocket till we're there," said Andrew quickly. "It might fall out. She always wears this. It's like putting Joanna herself in the farm."

"Like an effigy," said Simeon. "I hope it works, but it's only a trick to make Tailltu think she's getting the real thing."

"Yes," murmured Andrew. "Here, you carry the back end and I'll take the front."

As they skirted the yard and tramped through the orchard Andrew felt overwhelmed by the oppressive heat. It was an effort to move, let alone hurry. There were only one or two nights at most like this in an English summer, and one of them would have to be tonight.

"It's quiet," said Simeon, "still, no wind. I can't hear the trees and I've not heard one animal yet."

Andrew handed the model to Simeon to hold while he opened the gate. The gate swung against Simeon.

"Watch what you're doing. I nearly dropped it. You're meant to be looking for both of us. If you can't be bothered we might as well give up now."

"Shut up, Simeon. You always think you know everything but you don't," he said as he took his end of the model back.

Andrew was irritated by Simeon but he wasn't sure what they were arguing about. A splitting headache encircled his skull like a tight wire, hot and throbbing, stopping him from thinking clearly.

"My head hurts," he said by way of an apology.

"So does mine," said Simeon. "It's this awful heat."

Silently they trudged on round the wheatfield. Andrew's feet felt weighted to the ground, but as they reached the far gate a breeze began to blow. It was no cooling breeze, but a hot sticky flow of air. The corn stirred and rattled beside them.

"Listen to the rattle ... That corn's ripe enough," said Simeon.

The mown hayfield was easier-going but the model was surprisingly heavy and all the time they were climbing. As they came out on to the heathland, the wind blew up dust from the dry grass that clogged Andrew's nostrils and dried his eyes. The last light had faded.

"It's dark tonight, Simeon. It's all clouded over."

Heavy black clouds rolled across the sky above, layer upon layer of them, blocking out the moon. Andrew could hardly make out the path in front of him.

"I can't see a thing."

"Here. Let me lead," said Simeon.

"Let's have a rest first," said Andrew. "The model is a dead weight . . . I don't know how I carried it alone in town."

They set the model down between them. They were both panting.

"Will you know your way up through the wood? I got lost last night. I never got to the maze."

"Course I will. It makes no difference to me, night or day. If we carry this —" Simeon stopped. "Listen!"

Andrew listened to the swirling hot air and the rustling of the heath grasses around them. "What? I can't —"

"It's Sam."

"Are you sure?"

"I can hear him growling."

Andrew strained to listen. Sure enough he could catch a faint growl that he would never have noticed on his own. He jumped to his feet and peered into the darkness. "Sam's coming nearer. It must be Joanna."

"She can't have moved that great cupboard alone," said Simeon.

"I'm sure she's got out. Sam's trying to warn us."

Simeon leapt to his feet. Andrew strained, lifting the model up, and placed the front ends in the outstretched palms Simeon held out behind his back. Simeon moved forward with Andrew holding on behind. The growling was quite audible now.

"Run," said Simeon.

They broke into a stumbling trot, up under the beech trees. Gone was the previous heavy stillness. Now the hot wind stirred the leaves so that great rustlings and moanings broke overhead.

Simeon hesitated at the edge of the yews. "I've got no hand free to feel for branches. I can't go too fast."

Joanna had found her way in before. She was behind them still but she might overtake Simeon or get in faster than they could by a different route.

Andrew's head pounded and the steel band tightened. He could still hear the growling, but as far as he could tell it wasn't that close yet.

Painstakingly Simeon picked his way ahead, sliding his

feet gingerly in front of him. At times he ordered Andrew to hold the model while he felt a tree trunk or an overhanging branch. It all seemed so painfully slow.

Then, without warning, Andrew realised they were out on a path. He could hardly see further than his nose in front of him, but he could feel the track beneath his feet.

The track opened out, and Andrew could make out a wider, greyer vastness. They were there!

The yews that circled the maze loomed darkly, but the white chalk of the cut-away areas shone palely in the faint light. All around trees swayed and creaked, while up above dark clouds swirled and occasionally thinned to show a hint of yellow moon behind them.

"She's coming," Andrew panted. The growling was closer now than he had expected. "She's catching up on us!"

"Must have found another way," gasped Simeon. "Hold on tight to the back. I'm going into the maze."

Simeon fumbled his way along the paths of the maze. It took for ever, back and forward with so little progress. If they kept on at this rate, Joanna would soon catch them up.

At times they seemed so near to the dim square of grass and then they would move back on a curl of the path, close to where they had started out from. It was impossible to tell how near they were.

Andrew glanced back over his shoulder. "How far, Simeon?" He tried to control the rising panic in his voice.

"We're about halfway."

"Joanna's standing at the edge."

The thin, shadowy shape stood erect and still at the rim of the maze. As the shadow slid forward, Sam broke into a shrill whining, as he ran up and down outside the maze.

"She's coming in."

"Shut up. If you talk, I can't remember," Simeon said in a strangled voice.

"She's moving faster than us."

The wind was rising to a scream and the air rushing round them was stifling.

"I told you," shouted Simeon. "Don't hassle me. I can't go any faster."

"Try!"

"If I make a mistake, it'll be over. I'll never get it right."

Andrew bit the inside of his mouth. He wanted to yell out and warn Simeon. Joanna was moving forward rapidly and surely.

"Nearly there," panted Simeon.

Andrew's arms were ready to fall off. The model weighed more than he had ever imagined.

The path led back to the outer edges of the maze, while Joanna's path was in leaping distance of the grass. Simeon twisted round so abruptly that Andrew almost dropped his end of the model. He tasted blood in his mouth where he had bitten his lip to stop himself shouting, but now Simeon was leading straight back and – they were on the grass.

They laid the model at their feet. Andrew snatched open the front of the farmhouse and dug into his pocket for the locket. He laid it in the room that was Joanna's bedroom and snapped the front wall back into place. Then he spun round and watched Joanna.

She had hesitated, as if uncertain where to go next.

"She's stopped, Simeon."

"She can't have found her way right through to the grass before. Is she trying to work out the way?"

"Of course!" said Andrew. "She had to find out how to get to the grass square. That's why she kept coming up here – to work out the way. Once she's got to the grass, what will we do then?"

A great rumble roared overhead.

"Thunder," said Simeon. "Quick, leave it. Let's get out."

Andrew followed Simeon as he wound along the paths of the maze. Distant lightning lit up the sky as the rolls of thunder became louder and closer.

Sam whined pitifully from the edge.

They were level with Joanna when it came: a massive fork of lightning. It shot down and seemed to pinion the grove and shake the ground beneath them. It hurled the boys back against the massive trunk of an old yew. For a moment the whole grove was lit by a blinding blue light that seemed to pierce the centre of the grass square. Flames flared up, bright orange and yellow, and then died down as suddenly as they had come.

Andrew couldn't bear to watch the burning. Besides, his view was blocked by a great bundle in his arms.

"Let go of me, you ass," said Joanna.

All three sank back dazed and silent in the darkness until

a driving sheet of rain torrented down, drenching them back to their senses.

"I'm cold," said Joanna, shivering as she clutched hold of the boys. "Wouldn't Mum be mad if she knew we were out at night in a storm like this? It's exciting though, isn't it?"

Andrew stared at Joanna but he couldn't see her face. "Yes," he said lamely.

"What do you mean, yes?" said Joanna. "I think it's great! We should see if Beatrice has got a tent, then we could make an overnight camp on the heath."

"Yes."

"Oh come on, Andrew. Don't be so unenthusiastic. You've got to be a bit more adventurous. If she hasn't got a tent we could make one with sticks and blankets. You're good at that sort of thing. And we could make our own fire, and cook sausages and baked potatoes ... I'm really hungry. Have you two got anything to eat on you?"

Simeon sat in stupefied silence, but he reached in his pocket and pulled out a bag that rustled in his hand. "They're sherbet lemons and there's some cola balls at the bottom," he said.

"Better than nothing," said Joanna, popping one in her mouth. "Ugh! They're all sticky and dusty."

"It's been hot. They taste all right to me," said Simeon in an offended tone.

"They're lovely, Simeon, when you've licked the dust off. Here, Andrew, you try one. You don't mind, do you, Simeon?"

Andrew dug around at the bottom of the bag for a cola ball.

"Don't take all night!" said Joanna. "You've got to watch him, Simeon. He'll take two."

"How can I watch him?"

"You can count, can't you? There were fourteen sweets, weren't there, Simeon?"

"Well . . ."

"Yes there were. Count them." Simeon put his hand in the bag and smiled. "You're right. There's only ten now. One's missing."

"Honestly, I only had one!" shouted Andrew indignantly.

"You didn't."

"I did! Joanna, you're pretending!"

Joanna started to laugh. The laughter burst out of her as if it had been contained far too long. Simeon began to laugh too.

Andrew looked at them both, angry and tense after all they'd been through. Then Joanna's laugh worked through to him, as it had always done before, and he relaxed and smiled as if a dry, warm blanket had at last been wrapped round his freezing, wet shoulders. He pretended to hit out and thump Joanna. She rolled over giggling to the edge of the maze.

"Get off, you mad dog!" she shouted. Sam was standing over her, licking her face. Joanna pushed the dog playfully away and staggered to her feet. "Come on, you lot," she said. "We'd better get back before Beatrice notices we're missing. It's the harvest tomorrow."

The rain had stopped as suddenly as it had started.

"We can sleep late," said Simeon. "It will take a bit to dry this rain off in the morning. You can't cut the wheat when it's wet."

"I can't wait," said Joanna. "It's been so boring walking round and round each day. You should have seen me leap from my window – it was fun!"

"You jumped out of the window?" said Andrew.

"The door was stuck. Don't tell Beatrice. Anyone remember the way out of here?"

· Chapter Twelve ·

The following morning they were all down by eleven o'clock, after Bella had tried in vain to wake them every half hour. The corn was still not quite dry enough.

"Reckon we should give it another hour," said Gramps. "Just our luck to get a storm like that."

"It's cleared the air, Peter. We'll work all the more comfortably for it," said Beatrice.

Andrew edged round to where Simeon was standing beside Gramps. "Come on," he whispered. "Let's go and look."

"Can I come?" said Bella.

"No, it's too far."

"I'll come," said Joanna. "Where are you going?"

"No you won't, Joanna," said Beatrice firmly. "You were exhausted yesterday, like a wet rag. If you want to help us today, you'll take it easy and stay here."

"But I feel fine."

Beatrice looked at her sternly. Andrew wondered how Beatrice would get on with the real Joanna.

Simeon and he walked side by side up the track to the woods. They didn't need to talk. The sun was shining and after the storm all the birds of the heath seemed to be out swooping and singing in the bright, fresh air.

Andrew followed Simeon through the beeches and then

in and under the yews until they emerged in the grove at the edge of the maze.

"Ready? I'll go ahead," said Simeon.

"Do we need to? I mean it's all over now, isn't it, that Tailltu stuff?"

"I reckon so, but I only know my way to the grass by following the maze."

Andrew linked his arm through Simeon's. "Race you!" he said.

They ran straight across the maze ignoring the paths, stumbling over the chalk edges and laughing.

"Look!" said Andrew.

They were on the grass. Before them lay a pile of wet cinders. Simeon stooped down and ran his fingers through the black ashes.

"There's nothing left."

"It's completely burnt out," whispered Andrew, kneeling down close to Simeon, watching the ashes fall through Simeon's fingers. All that work, the plan to help Dad, had been destroyed in so few seconds.

"Can you see any gold?" said Simeon. "I can't find a trace of metal."

"No. It's gone."

With their arms round each other's shoulders they meandered out of the beechwood together. Someone was walking out of the hayfield, up the track towards them. Andrew stopped and shaded his eyes from the sun.

"Come on," he shouted, pulling Simeon with him.

"What is it?" complained Simeon.

"It's Mum!"

She looked tired, with the pallor of someone who didn't get outside much, but she was smiling.

"You didn't tell me," said Andrew.

"I did. I said the next free Monday."

"Is it Monday? I've lost track of the days."

"I'm not surprised. It's like another world here," she sighed wistfully. "Dad has found a job. He sent a message – something about knowing he can rely on you. He's working so hard he hasn't got a minute to write."

She stared out over the field of golden corn to where Gramps was tinkering with the combine.

"Bella wants to stay with Beatrice for ever! But you might have a word with Joanna. She's so tactless, saying that she'll be bored with the country once the harvest is over and she can't wait to get back to town. Beatrice looked quite hurt."

Mum gazed out over the fields and heath as if she could scarcely take in what lay before her. She turned and smiled at Andrew, and already he could see some of the weariness lifting.

"And Beatrice! I knew she would enjoy having you all for the summer – but she's a different woman. I'd never have believed it. She says you and Simeon have been making a wonderful model of the farm. You must show it to me . . . "

Andrew opened the gate into the orchard. He couldn't trust himself to speak.

"Oh that," said Simeon, "that was just a trial model. We're going to start on the real thing after the harvest, aren't we, Andrew?"